The Crackajack Pony

Books by Mebane Holoman Burgwyn

THE CRACKAJACK PONY
HUNTERS' HIDEOUT
TRUE LOVE FOR JENNY
MOONFLOWER
RIVER TREASURE
LUCKY MISCHIEF
PENNY ROSE

The
CRACKAJACK
PONY

Mebane Holoman Burgwyn

Illustrated by Dale Payson

J. B. Lippincott Company

Philadelphia　　　　　　　New York

To Mary, Dan, Michele, and Anne Maria
who came to Occoneechee

CONTENTS

The Crackajack Pony

1

THE SECRET

Cliff stood, alone and angry, on the hot pavement in front of his home as Jim and Bud moved away from him down the street. He searched the corners of his mind for some word that would stop them. He knew that the boys might be headed for trouble yet he yearned to be with them.

The boys walked slowly as if they had no real plans but their secret destination was the railroad yards beyond the small park two blocks west. Cliff's arms hung help-lessly by his side as he stood in the blazing sunlight and watched them go. Sweat had popped out on his sturdy body beneath the yellow T-shirt and the tight denim shorts that hugged his slender hips.

Halfway down the block Mrs. Ellerbee had her sprinkler going in her small yard and it was slinging huge drops of water across parched grass as it whirled. Two of the Mead children, clad in brief panties, were taking turns running through the glittering spray of water, shrieking when the cold drops hit their bare skin. Old Mr. Brown sat on his porch across the street, oblivious to the noise and the heat, thinking his silent secret thoughts and rocking away the hours of time and boredom.

For a moment Cliff thought of calling the boys back and telling them his secret but he thrust the idea from him. He considered running after them, but he could not forget the sharp words of warning that Daddy had spoken when the police had forbidden the boys on West End Boulevard to play at the railroad yards anymore because of what had happened to Jim and Bud.

Jim and Bud Elam, whose home was farther down the block, had lived through a narrow escape. Cliff watched the two boys now, wondering how they dared go back, his admiration of their daring spirit making him feel desperately alone. He wanted to be with them, wanted to share the adventures of this morning.

Bud was a broad and heavy boy who moved and thought slowly and he was relaxed and good-natured, but it was Jim who excited Cliff. Jim was a dark and winsome boy with a lean face and a long upper lip that protruded slightly. He had bright eyes that constantly scanned the scene about him in his hungry search for adventure. It was easy to get caught in the trap of Jim's tongue. He could argue the horns off a billy goat and could melt the heart right out of a boy who tried to say no. Cliff knew how it was to feel his knees grow weak with anticipation when Jim suggested a bold idea.

He knew how it must have been last fall when Jim coaxed Bud to climb aboard the boxcar loaded with empty beer bottles when no one was looking. The car had been locked by accident while they were still inside and then hooked onto a fast westbound train. No degree of screaming and yelling had been loud enough for anyone to hear. The car had been taken all the way to Milwaukee, Wisconsin, where it was backed onto a side track and left for two weeks.

All of the neighbors on West End Boulevard had mourned the strange disappearance of the boys. Many had given up hope that they would ever be found and then one day the car had been opened. There the boys were, half dead from hunger, and sick from draining the beer bottles just to stay alive. They returned to school, heroes, enveloped with the glory of their escape, celebrated because of their miraculous return from eternity where so many had imagined them.

Cliff who lived next door to Jim had been among his admirers and he had enjoyed many hours with Jim but there were unhappy times when he felt excluded from Jim's activities, days when Jim moved away from him into a secret world he shared with other boys, moments when Jim cut him off and made him feel alone.

This was such a moment. It was Jim who had refused to play ball in the park today, Jim who had suggested going back to the railroad yards, and Jim who had called him a sissy when he said he wouldn't go.

The lonely moment seemed intolerable. Even worse than being left alone was the sting of Jim's scornful words that still rang in Cliff's ears. Sissy? Nobody had ever called him a sissy before. A stifling surge of anger swept over Cliff.

"I don't care what you say," he called loud enough for them to hear but careful to keep his voice low enough not to be heard by Mrs. Ellerbee. The boys paid no attention but kept on walking.

"I don't care what you say," he repeated, slightly louder.

Jim turned around then and walked backward for a few steps. "Cliff is a chicken," he called back softly in a sing-song voice. "Cliff is a chicken."

Real fury rose within Cliff, now. He clinched his fists at his sides and searched wildly for something to say to Jim. Something that would hurt. Something that would stop both of them in their tracks. They weren't really so smart. He knew a lot of things they didn't know. The secret that he had been keeping from the boys for several weeks boiled inside him. If he told them they might stop and come back. Jim would give his eyeteeth to know this secret. But they were getting farther and farther away.

For a brief instant the secret hung balanced on his lips. Then, before he knew it, the words were tumbling out.

"I'm going to get a pony," he shouted.

The boys stopped. Jim and Bud turned around, surprise written on their faces. Cliff's satisfaction with their response was sweet, but it lasted only an instant for Jim laughed scornfully.

"Yeah," he said. "I bet. Where do you think you're going to put him?"

Bud laughed then and started walking backward, too. "In his pocket, I guess," he said and then he smiled, pleased with himself. "He'll put the pony in his pocket."

Now, Jim was smiling.

"That's right," he said. "That's a good place for a

Cracker Jack prize pony. Cliff's too chicken to ride a real pony. He's scared."

Bud echoed Jim's words. "Yeah, Cliff's too chicken to do anything but play ball in the park."

With that, Cliff's ears began to pound and fury tingled throughout his body. These were the best friends he had on the block. It could not be possible that they had turned on him this way.

The boys turned again and began to saunter on toward the park and the railroad yards beyond. Cliff watched them go, his heart beating hard against his chest, his lips pressed tight against his teeth and the sting of tears rising behind his eyelids.

"Okay, go on," he shouted. "You blasted big-headed bums." His voice was loud and angry. There was no effort to keep the tone down now.

He heard the front screen door slam. His mother came out onto the porch. She was slender and trim in the bright blue housedress that fitted close to her body. A scarlet ribbon across her head above her high brow held her dark curly hair pulled away from her warm brown eyes. She looked fresh and cool in spite of the intense heat.

"Cliff Morgan. What is that you're saying? Aren't you ashamed of yourself? Shouting ugly names like that out on the street for everybody to hear."

Cliff stood quite still, anger at the boys and frustration over being scolded mingling now within him.

"Come here." His mother waited on the tiny porch while Cliff allowed his body to relax and forced his steps back toward her.

"What's your trouble?"

Cliff hung his head and said nothing. He had no intention of telling Mama that the boys were going down to the railroad tracks. They might call him a sissy but they would never call him a tattletale.

"What were you fussing about?" Cliff noted the dangerous tone and his mind moved from one reason to another that he could give her without telling on the boys.

"Tell me, Cliff. What were you yelling about? I'm downright embarrassed to have you standing out in the street shouting like a banshee."

Cliff threw his mother a sidelong glance. "What's a banshee?" he said with a half smile, hoping to divert her.

"Don't get funny with me," Mama said. "I want to know more about this fuss."

"They're just so biggety," Cliff said.

"That's no reason for you to lose your temper and yell all up and down the street."

Cliff turned his head aside to hide the feeling of real frustration that welled up within him. Everything was wrong. The boys were mad at him because he had refused to go with them. He had told them his secret which he had wanted to be a surprise when the pony came, and they weren't even excited. In fact, they hadn't even believed him. They had just made fun of the whole idea. Now Mama was mad because he had yelled a stupid old name at them and he couldn't tell her why.

"Your daddy will be upset with you when he comes home this afternoon if he knows you were fighting with the boys. You should try to get along with your friends."

"They're not such good friends," said Cliff. "They laughed at me when I told them I was going to get a pony."

He looked directly at his mother and saw her expression

change. Her bright face that had been severe, almost angry, softened now. Her full lips closed in a gentle smile.

"Oh, Cliff," she said. "I hate so badly for you to be disappointed about the pony. You know you can't be sure about it and I told you not to tell the boys until you were. It isn't easy to win a pony in a contest. There were lots of people trying to get that pony. You know that."

Cliff nodded miserably. She had told him that a hundred times.

"But I worked the puzzle out and then I sold all the seed they sent me," he said.

"I know." Mama's tone was gentle now. "But they still have to pick a name out of all those who sold the seed and yours will be in the box with thousands of other names."

"I've still got a chance," said Cliff stubbornly. "I thought I might hear today."

"The closing date was more than a week ago, Cliff," Mama said. "You should have heard by now if you had won. And where on earth would you keep a pony even if you did win?" She looked at the narrow strip of lawn between the small porch and the city street where cars sped east and west.

Cliff sighed. They had been over all this before. "Daddy said he'd find a place for the pony if I won him," he said.

"I don't know how he thinks we can keep a pony in the back yard. There's hardly room for the vegetables now, and Paul and Wesley must have a place to play. Sometimes your daddy acts like he's no more than twelve years old either."

There was a loud crash inside where Cliff's two little brothers were playing. She threw up her hands. "Paul and Wesley are into something," she said. She went back into the house. Cliff sat down on the steps, glad that she had forgotten the fuss and had left him alone. His limbs felt as heavy as lead.

He pressed the back of his head against the lacy wrought-iron columns, chipped and rusted now from years of exposure to the heat and cold of city weather. He looked at the dried wisps of grass on the tiny lawn, not much bigger than Daddy's station wagon, and then across the scorching hot paved street at the small squares of lawn area spread out before the solid line of identical brick houses that stretched in monotonous order as far as he could see. Small porches shaded doorways from the hot glare of June sunlight, but even those which had scanty vines growing feebly over a latticework of string could not shut out the blazing heat.

Mrs. James, three doors down on the right, had red geraniums on the railing of her porch, and her gray cat, Whiskers, sat sunning himself beside them. Cliff looked at the cat and sighed again deeply. His fingers itched to feel the soft fur and warm purring body of the animal. Mama didn't care much for animals, especially cats, and especially cats that stayed in the house, and Mrs. James wasn't very friendly either so he did not get to play with Whiskers or any other animal very often.

Cliff sighed once more and his eyes followed the street until they touched the green trees in the park two blocks west of his home.

Without thinking, he rose to his feet and began to walk slowly toward them. He felt smothered between the old red brick buildings and the scorching pavement and the pale sun-drenched sky overhead. He thought dismally about how hard it was to keep things going smoothly with the boys. And Mama lost her temper more now than she used to when they lived in Raleigh, North Carolina, with Grandma. Of course, that was before Paul got sick and had such a hard time getting over it. Mama had stayed so worried about his little brother that she still fussed over him if he even started to sneeze. Cliff thought about Daddy who was hardly ever at home because of having to visit other cities to sell medical supplies. Mama said he would be home this afternoon but even this failed to lift Cliff's spirits.

He reached the corner across from the park. The trees were tall and gaunt, the grass beneath them parched and brown. It was not much of a park compared to the lush green fields and woods on the farm Uncle Ed owned in North Carolina, but it was better than nothing, Cliff thought.

He ran across the street until he reached the grassy spot beneath the tall oak trees that cast filtered shadows over the park. Here, his steps grew slower and he moved a short distance until he was in the deepest part of the shade. Then he flung himself full length on the ground. The crushed blades of grass touched his face and the hot summer air moved lightly over his back, but beneath his body, pressed hard against the earth, Cliff felt the heavy pulse of the city that throbbed like the unhappy pounding of his own heart.

2

GOOD NEWS

For a long time Cliff lay quite still, face down, but finally the tension of his body began to leave him and he felt easier inside. He rolled over on his back and looked up into the trees. The summer wind played softly through the leaves, and patterns of sunlight and shadow fell across his face. When he closed his eyes he could see colors that changed from brilliant red to yellow and then gray. Patches of sunlight moved like a hot spotlight over his body.

He remembered how he had lain this way along the riverbank of Uncle Ed's farm in North Carolina when he had visited there once, how beautiful the green trees looked bending down to touch the reddish water of the Roanoke, how soft and fleecy the clouds were against the deep blue of the sky. He had hoped he might go back to see Uncle Ed again this year but Uncle Ed had gotten sick and only three weeks ago Daddy had gone down to North Carolina for his funeral. Since then, Daddy had stayed down there most of the time signing papers and looking after things that Uncle Ed had left.

It was sad to think he would never see Uncle Ed again. Uncle Ed had been quieter than Daddy but he knew lots of things about the woods and animals and snakes. He had let Cliff feed the chickens and gather eggs and when they went fishing at Blue Hole Mill Pond he taught Cliff how to know exactly when to pull the line after his cork bobbed under the water.

"If you've got patience to wait for that second, you'll get that old fish every time," Uncle Ed had told him.

He thought of the big farm a mile below Uncle Ed's farm where Mr. Taylor raised ponies. He thought of the Beaver Dam, the wild plums, the Venus's-flytraps that grew along the edge of the woods beside the river and the bobwhites that called to each other across the fields. He thought of all the ways Uncle Ed had helped to make the country seem like magic to a city boy.

Cliff sighed. Uncle Ed was gone. He would not be visiting there anymore. Instead, here he lay dreaming about the country and underneath it all wishing for a pony that Mama was sure he would never win.

"I've got to keep hoping," he thought. Daddy said a man might not get all he wished for but he couldn't get anything without wanting it a lot and then working hard for it. If hard work would help he should have a good chance to win the pony. He had not thought it would be

so hard when he first saw the puzzle in the paper with
the pony beside it.

"WORK THE PUZZLE AND WIN THE PONY!"
the ad had stated, but when he sent the puzzle in with
the correct solution, the company had sent him a box of
seed to sell. During the winter he had walked up and
down the blocks around him until his legs felt too tired
to move. Not many of the ladies used their small back
yards to plant vegetables like Mama did and it had taken
him weeks to find people who would buy all of his seed,
but he had finally sold them.

The company had allowed him to keep four dollars of
the money but the other six dollars had been sent back
along with a number. Now, if his number had been drawn
from the box last week when the contest closed he would
win the pony. Daddy said he would probably get a letter
telling him if he had won and the pony would come later
by truck or on the train.

Cliff sat up suddenly. It must be getting close to twelve
o'clock and the postman came at twelve. The letter might
come today. He'd better get home.

He jumped to his feet and brushed dried grass from his
clothes as he moved across the park toward the street.
When he crossed the street at the corner of the block he
saw the station wagon in front of his house.

"Daddy's home early," he said half aloud and, as hot
as it was, he quickened his pace so that he was almost
running when he reached the house. Daddy was home
and things would be better now. Somehow, they always
were when Daddy was there.

He burst through the house, down the long musty-
smelling hall into the kitchen that Mama had tried to

brighten with yellow paint. Daddy and Mama were sitting at the round table but they looked so serious that Cliff stopped short just inside the door. He could hear Paul and Wesley playing in the sandpile outside the kitchen window.

"Hi, Daddy," he said and he moved toward the table slowly. Daddy was a big man with broad shoulders and large muscular hands. He had played basketball in college and had the clean-cut look of an athlete. His dark hair grew crisply up from a wide high brow and his face had an open expression that was bright and alert. He didn't usually hug Cliff anymore when he came home, but this time he reached out a long arm as Cliff drew close to his chair and pulled him against his side.

"How're things?" he asked. "You look like you've grown another inch this week." His hand moved up Cliff's strong back and clasped Cliff's upper arm in his big hand. "Need to work on those muscles."

"I'm okay," said Cliff. He wanted to tell his daddy how much he missed him and how glad he was to have him back at home, but it was hard to say things like that so he smiled happily at him and dropped his hand on Daddy's shoulder so he could feel the strength of muscles beneath his white shirt.

"What's the news with you?" Daddy asked.

Cliff was thoughtful for a moment. Then he spoke with words that tumbled out. "Would you call me a sissy fellow?" he asked.

Daddy turned to face him. He pushed Cliff away from him a little and looked searchingly at the dark brown eyes in which, even now, at this serious moment, laughter seemed to sparkle. He looked at the strong angle of Cliff's

face, at the wide firm mouth that broke easily into a
sunny smile upon any provocation, and at the positive
direct way Cliff confronted him.

"I can't see a single sissy inch," Daddy said. "In fact,
I think you are absolutely crackajack. Why do you ask?"

Cliff made a face, remembering Jim's comment about
the Cracker Jack prize pony. He wanted to tell Daddy
about the boys, where they had gone, and how they had
laughed about the pony but he knew he couldn't talk
about that. Then he saw the troubled look on Mama's
face. She opened her mouth as if to say something and
Cliff spoke quickly to head off any comment she might
be planning to make about his fuss this morning.

"I haven't heard whether I won the pony yet," he said.

"Well, it's still a little bit early, don't you think? Maybe
you'll hear in a day or two." He pulled his arm away from
Cliff then and said, "Come around here and sit down.
Mama and I have been talking about some news that you
might like to hear almost as well as winning the pony."

Cliff's quick eyes looked at Mama again. There was a
slight frown between her dark liquid eyes and she seemed
thoughtful—not angry. Maybe worried just a little.

He sat down across the table from Daddy, mystified
by the announcement of news that was good but made
Mama look so thoughtful. For a moment the kitchen was
quiet except for the sound of chicken frying on the stove
and, outside, Paul's thin voice which floated through the
window.

"Hey, Wes, get your truck out of the way. Mine's
coming through the tunnel." He made the sound of a
motor running at full speed.

"We think we will be moving soon, Cliff." Daddy's
voice fell quietly in the room.

"Moving?" said Cliff. He felt his body freeze. He hated moving to new places—having to make new friends—getting adjusted to a different city, a different house, a different school. "Moving? Where?"

"We're thinking of moving to Uncle Ed's farm."

Cliff's mouth dropped open and his heart gave a wild joyous leap.

"To Uncle Ed's farm?" He could not believe what he was hearing. "Honest? You really mean it? You mean we're moving there to live? All the time?" Joy shone in his eyes.

"Yes. Uncle Ed left the farm to me and we're thinking it might be good for you boys if we moved there, especially for Paul. Would you like that?"

"Oh, golly. Would I like it'" He stood up and walked around the table and then sat down again. He felt excitement running all through his body. "Will we be going soon?"

"As soon as we can get things straightened out here," said Daddy.

"How long?" Cliff asked.

"As soon as Mama can get organized. Maybe a week—or two weeks."

Cliff looked at Mama then and he understood the thoughtful look. She wasn't happy about moving. That was why she looked so worried.

"Don't you want to go, Mama?"

Her eyes suddenly filled with tears and she rose from the table and went to the stove without speaking. Cliff looked at Daddy.

"Doesn't she want to live there?"

"Well, she's not as sure as we are, Cliff. She's not used to the country and she doesn't know whether she'll like it or not." Daddy stood up, then, his big body, light and muscular, seeming to fill the little kitchen.

"Oh, Mama, I know you'll like it. It's a lot cooler there and you can sit out on the porch at night."

"And listen to the frogs," said Mama. She furiously stirred something that was cooking in a pot on the stove. She did not look around but Cliff could tell that her voice was unsteady as if she were still crying.

"Frogs sound good when you get used to them," Cliff said. "And you can have a whole lot better garden. And there'll be chickens."

"I can't stand the smell of chickens," said Mama.

"You don't seem to mind them fried," said Daddy laughing. He put his arms around her waist and swung her around to face him.

Mama laughed then and she wiped the corner of her eyes with her apron. "It's just that I was born and bred in the city," she said to Daddy. "The idea of living in the country makes me nervous. But I've told you that I'll try it. Ed left the farm to you and I know that somebody has to take over his crop and harvest it. Paul has been sick so much I'm sure the country air and sunshine will be like a tonic for him." She tried to make her voice sound cheerful but Cliff could tell that she was making a big effort to keep her words steady.

Daddy laughed as if he did not notice. "I'm not really worried about you," he said. "I know you'll be all right." He turned to Cliff. "It's been a long time since I've farmed, Cliff. It will take a lot of money and some hard work and I'll need you to help me." He walked over to the back door and looked out at the little boys. "I'll have to keep on with my job for a few weeks until my company finds another man to replace me and then I will be at home nearly all the time." He turned and came back to stand beside Mama at the stove. "It will be a big change for us. We'll have to help Mama get used to it, Cliff."

Mama spoke again, her back still turned as she worked at the stove. "I've said that I will go and I intend to do my part. I'll listen to the frogs and smell the chickens and make the best of it."

Cliff looked at Mama's slender back, at the way she held her shoulders, proud and straight, and he knew she meant what she said. He felt a lump rise in his own throat.

"Oh, Mama, I just know you'll like it. I'll help you with your work, too. I'll feed the chickens and mow the grass. I'll—" Feeling sorry for Mama just did not keep his happiness down. It rose like a flood inside of him. He could not sit still any longer. He got up and walked around the kitchen again and as he did so he heard the postman's footsteps on the porch.

The pony! Now he'd have a place to keep the pony. He raced down the hall toward the front door and reached inside the mailbox, drawing out four letters the postman had left.

There were two bills and a letter for his father and a letter for Mama from Grandma, but not a word about the pony.

3

PLEA FOR A LETTER

During the following days it was hard for Cliff to control his happiness. It burst from his lips when he was walking from his room to the kitchen, and he whistled when he walked down the street as he went to the grocery store for Mama. He awoke each morning to find Mama already at work in the kitchen or dining room, packing up things that she hardly ever used. He was eager to help her. Sometimes he would fix his own breakfast or cook an egg for Paul and Wesley while she worked at something else, or he would take the boys outside while she prepared their dinner. When she put the little boys to bed for a nap in the afternoon or at night after supper, he would help her wrap the good china in newspapers and pack it away in boxes.

When he handed her a cup or a vase from the big cabinet where she kept her best things she would stop and tell him how she came to have this.

"Your Aunt Sue gave that to me just before she died," Mama told him one evening when he gave her the big cut-glass bowl. "She said Uncle Ed and she hardly ever used it and she wanted someone in Uncle Ed's family to enjoy it because it was so beautiful." Cliff was careful to make sure she had it securely in her hands before he turned it loose. Mama always used it on Christmas Day. She served ambrosia made of fresh oranges, sugar, and fresh grated coconut with red cherries and holly leaves to decorate it.

He asked her questions about Aunt Sue and Uncle Ed, partly to keep her mind off the friends she had made here in the city and all the things she enjoyed doing, but mainly, because he loved to hear about Uncle Ed and Aunt Sue who had died soon after Uncle Ed built the farmhouse in the Occoneechee Neck.

Once she asked him how he felt about leaving his friends and he thought about that for awhile before he answered her.

"We've moved so many times, I guess I've gotten sort of used to it now, Mama. Some places it's easier to make friends than it is in others."

"How about here?" she asked him.

Cliff thought about Jim—how he was sometimes so friendly and then how he would act as if he had never been a friend. He thought about the way the boys would play with him sometimes and then would move off into a secret world that they would not share with him. He

thought about the lonely way this made him feel, but he
did not want to tell Mama about it. The ache of it was
a feeling that he kept locked tightly inside himself. He
sometimes wondered if this was a problem for all boys
who had to move from place to place a lot.

"We haven't been here long enough for me to feel
real close to any of the boys. They don't always like to
do the things I like to do."

It was the closest he could come to telling her how it
really was. He kept handing her pieces of china but his
thoughts were on Jim and the other boys who had looked
at him with unbelieving envy when he told them that he
was going to live on a farm where he could ride his pony
all he wanted to.

He wondered if there would be any boys living close to
them on the farm. He had not stayed with Uncle Ed long
enough to meet boys living in Occoneechee Neck and as
hard as he tried he could not remember how close other
houses were or how many of them there were, except for
Mr. Taylor who raised the ponies.

As if she had been reading his thoughts, Mama said,
"It isn't easy to move into a new place and make new
friends, especially if you stand off and wait for other boys
to be nice to you."

Cliff looked at Mama curiously. Sometimes, he thought,
her brain actually moved inside his. It was almost scary.

"How do you get fellows to accept you when you're
new and strange? You can't just go up to them and say,
'Hey, you guys, I want to be your friend.' "

Mama laughed in the gay way she had when she was
amused, and then she became serious.

"No, you can't do it that way but there are lots of
things you can do."

"Like what?" Cliff stopped wrapping the cup he held in his hand and looked at her.

"Well, you can be friendly without being forward or pushy. You can meet people at least halfway. Maybe even go out of your way to be pleasant."

"Suppose after you've been friendly they turn around and belt you with some smart idea or answer," Cliff asked.

Mama looked thoughtful. "I know that young people can often be as cruel as grown-ups, Cliff. Sometimes it's because they have poor manners and sometimes it's because they aren't old enough or sensitive enough to think about other people's feelings."

"I know that may be why," said Cliff, "but I want to know how you act when that happens."

"Well, first of all, I think you have to be strong enough to take a few blows along the way without letting it get you down. Everybody gets hurt sometimes and most anyone can wear a chip on his shoulder if he wants to be that way."

"What does that mean—wearing a chip on your shoulder?"

"That means feeling sorry for yourself all the time—letting your feelings get hurt too easily. It's just as if you put a chip on your shoulder and dared someone to knock it off all the time."

Cliff nodded. "I can see that," he said. "But how do you act when somebody says mean things or walks away when you're trying to be friendly?" He was persistent.

"A little laughter helps at times like that," Mama said. "But I guess the best thing to do is to keep a level head—to remember how many things you have going for you—to think of something you have that you can be glad about—things like what kind of person you are, that you

are honest, you have courage, that you do what you think
is right. If you think about these things instead of feeling
sorry for yourself, pretty soon what the other fellows say
doesn't matter and they'll respect you more than if you
yell and scream ugly names at them."

Cliff smiled a little at that, remembering how he had
lost his temper with Jim and the other boys.

"Sometimes when a person is mad or disappointed or
worried about something he will lash out and try to hurt
someone else. That's what you were doing when the boys
teased you because you wouldn't go to the railroad yards
with them."

Mama was reaching into the cabinet for more dishes as
she spoke and Cliff stared at her in amazement. She
knew! All the time she knew! She understood how it was!

Cliff worked thoughtfully, remembering Mama's words
during the days that passed. He thought a lot about what
she had said and he thought about Mama, too, and how
she felt about moving and leaving the attractive friends
who came to see her, but she did not talk about it. He
was conscious of her reservation about moving and he
worried about it some, but he kept thinking, "I know she
will like it after she has been there for a while. I'll do
everything I can to help her get used to it."

At night when Daddy would come home after being on
the job all day they would sit around the kitchen table
and talk about the farm and how they would work things
out. Several times Daddy went to the farm to take part of
their furniture in his station wagon and once he and
Mama spent a whole day there getting the house cleaned
up, leaving Cliff and the boys at home with Mrs. Sakow-
sky who came over to stay with them. When they came
back they talked about the house and the buildings out-

side, what had been planted and how tall the cotton was, and how nice it would be to have fresh corn. Cliff felt pure joy mounting inside him.

He thought about the pony, too, and visualized how it would be to have a pony that he could ride whenever he wished.

"Is there a good stable where I can keep my pony?" he asked. "I mean the pony I might get," he added as he saw Mama's change of expression.

"There is a good stable for a pony, Cliff," Daddy said. "And plenty of hay in the barn."

Mama sighed. "I don't know why you keep encouraging him," she said to Daddy.

"Because a man has got to have hope," Daddy said.

"Even when he knows he may be disappointed?" Mama asked.

"Even then," said Daddy. "That's part of learning, too."

Mama sighed again. "I wish he could hear, once and for all time about that pony," she said.

"Maybe I could write and ask them what's happened," said Cliff.

Daddy thought that was a good idea and in a matter of moments they had worked out a letter that sounded very official and businesslike to Cliff.

Dear Sir:

Recently I entered a contest for a pony which was conducted by your firm. I sent in a correct solution to your puzzle and received the seed which you requested that I sell. I sold the seed and sent in to you the amount of money you specified. I understood that the winner would be announced within a week after the close of the contest. It has now been over two weeks and I have heard nothing from you. I am very anxious to know whether or not I have won the pony. Please send me word about this as soon as possible as I am moving to the new address given below within the next week.

Sincerely yours,
Cliff Morgan

Cliff addressed the letter and handed it personally to the postman when he came the next day.

"I hope you hurry and bring me an answer to this," he said. "We don't have but five more days here and I sure would like to know if I'm going to get that pony before I leave."

"I'll do everything I can to rush it right out, Cliff," the postman said. "And if a letter comes after you're gone, I'll see to it myself that the letter is sent right on to you."

Cliff watched him walk down the street with the letter and he felt a tremendous surge of hope rising within him.

"Oh, please, please, please," he said half aloud. "I've got a place to put him and a place to ride him. Please bring me a letter saying that I've won that pony."

4

A VISITOR

It seemed forever until the day that the big truck came and the men started moving everything out of the house. Cliff found it difficult to stay out in the sandpile with Paul and Wesley to keep them out of the way for Mama. He kept going back into the house to see what was going on.

He watched the men take down his bed and move the chest of drawers out of the dark little room he had shared with Paul.

"Be careful with that box," he cautioned one of the movers. "I put my model horses and pictures in there."

"That's my business—being careful, Sonny," he told Cliff. "That's what your daddy's paying me for."

The house seemed more and more strange. Cliff's voice rang when he spoke in the empty rooms and he was glad when the last box and the last piece of furniture were loaded safely in the truck.

The car was packed with boxes and suitcases and Mama had a big picnic basket filled with fried chicken, biscuits, cake, and fruit so they would have plenty to eat while they were moving in and getting the house straight. Mama was very quiet as they moved things out but Daddy was cheerful and full of fun.

Daddy locked the door after they had taken a quick look around to see that nothing had been left and they climbed into the station wagon for the long trip.

Cliff sat in the back between Paul and Wesley. The picnic basket was on the floor below Wesley's short fat legs. Wesley's face was round and full of mischief. His full mouth turned up at the corners and his dark eyes were often teasing. He talked very little except to echo Paul's words.

"Keep your feet off the basket, Wesley," Cliff cautioned his little brother.

"Sit down, Paul. You've got to help me look for the house when we get there."

"I want to look at the truck," Paul said and he continued to look out the back window at the big truck which was to follow Daddy as he led the way. Cliff looked at his six-year-old brother whose face and body were still thin as a result of the long illness he had suffered and he smiled at Paul. Paul often got his way just because everyone had to smile at his delicate sweetness of expression.

Cliff noticed Mama looking back when they drove off,

but he was so excited that he felt no regrets at all. He saw Bill Brown and Bud as they passed the Elam house and they waved back to him but he caught no glimpse of Jim. He breathed a big sigh as if to release all the pent-up emotions he felt and then he crossed his arms over his chest, hugging his excitement close to himself.

It was almost three o'clock when they turned off the main highway onto the smaller paved road that led to the Occoneechee Neck.

"How far is it, now, Daddy?" Paul asked for the fifteenth time.

"Only seven more miles, Paul," Daddy said. "We'll be there soon."

Cliff shifted Wesley's damp little head that lay in his lap. "May I wake him up, now, Mama?"

"No. Let him sleep as long as he will. He'll be cross if he doesn't get his nap out," she said.

"The truck's not coming. It's not turning behind us," Paul called out, distress in his voice.

Cliff twisted his body around the best that he could with Wesley's head still lying on his lap and saw the truck turn onto the smaller road.

"Yes, it is, too, Paul. You've said that every time we've gone around a single curve."

"Well, sometimes it gets so far behind," Paul said.

The miles flew by now. They passed a store and a cotton gin, then an old building that once was a schoolhouse and a moment later they turned to the right onto the long dirt road that led to Uncle Ed's house a half mile away. Cliff could already see the huge oak trees and before he knew it they had come to a dirt road that ran east and west along the river woods. They turned to the left onto the lane which passed in front of the low rambling house that Uncle Ed had built for his wife who had not lived to enjoy it very long. Daddy stopped the station wagon.

The house was painted white with green shutters and it nestled beneath huge willow oaks and masses of pink and lavender crepe myrtle trees. Land spilled out on each side and in front of the oak grove which offered cool and restful shade. Behind the house were barns and farm buildings and beyond them was a small corn field separating the barns from the deep woods that fringed the Roanoke River. The small path in front of the house followed the westward curve of the woods that bordered the river for more than a mile from this point down to the great bend where it circled about the land of Occoneechee Neck and flowed back east toward the Albemarle Sound.

Cliff shook Wesley and waited impatiently while his little brother sat up slowly and looked sleepily about him.

"Look, Wes," Cliff said. "It's our new home." Paul was already out of the car and Cliff could wait no longer. He climbed over Wesley's legs and bounded toward the low white fence and the ivy-bordered walk that led to the large screened porch.

At the steps he paused and looked back.

"Go ahead," Daddy called. "The screen door's open. I'm coming with the key."

Cliff stepped onto the porch and looked about him. He had not remembered how beautiful it was. A cushioned glider and white wicker chairs gave the porch the appearance of a wide cool living room. There were growing plants in red pots on the white tables and a large grass rug covered the floor. Cliff followed Daddy through the open front door.

The large, paneled living room was completely furnished with things that Uncle Ed had left and furniture that Daddy had brought from home. There was the good sofa that Mama would not let them put their feet on, the old desk, polished and shining, and Daddy's easy chair between the window and the fireplace.

Daddy pushed up the window on the west side of the room and immediately a soft breeze whisked through the room lifting the clean white organdy curtains that Mama had put up the day she had spent here with Daddy.

He turned to see Mama coming in with her arms full of clothes. He ran toward her.

"Let me take them, Mama," he said.

"Bring them in here," she said. "This is where your daddy and I will stay." She opened a door to the right of the living room which led to a large room that was empty.

"Just hang those in the closet, Cliff, and I'll show you where your room will be."

He hung the clothes and then followed her back into the living room out into a little back hall, past the middle room where he had slept when he visited Uncle Ed, and back toward the last bedroom which had been the best company room.

"The middle room is Paul and Wesley's," Mama told him. "I thought you'd like to be back here in this room where you can look out toward the fields and the back yard."

Cliff looked in at the large room that faced northeast. He drew a deep breath of delight. A room all his own! There would be lots of space for his double bed and his chest of drawers, his bookcase, and the desk where he kept all his most treasured possessions. He'd put that here beside the east window. He moved toward the window and looked out onto the sight of broad fields already green with peanut vines that spread like a carpet over the earth.

A low fence ran along beside his window to a higher fence across the back yard. Between the fence and the peanut field was a path leading from the road in front of the house to a gate that opened into the barnyard.

Cliff walked to the back window and looked out at the grassy lawn where there was a swing and a sandpile under the trees. Beyond the high plank fence which cut off the view of the barnyard he could hear the sound of metal clanging against metal.

"Who's out there?" he asked.

"It's probably Hoke Harris," Mama said. "He lives about a half mile down the lane and he's going to help Daddy with the farm work until Daddy can give up his work with the company."

"I want to see what he's doing," Cliff said.

"Well, you can have a look around the house and then you can take the boys out and show them where things are outside while Daddy and I help the men get things placed in the house."

Cliff went back into the hallway. There was a small bathroom at the back of the hall beside his room. A doorway across the hall from his room led onto a screened back porch where there was a big white dining table and white chairs with tall ladder-backs. The dining room was between the porch and the living room. At the far end of the porch was the kitchen which had light paneled cabinets and yellow cabinet tops. There was a smaller table here.

Cliff stood for a moment looking at all of it. Everything in the house looked clean and neat and even more beautiful than he had imagined.

"I guess it makes a difference," he thought, "when you know you'll be living here all the time."

He heard Mama urge Wesley to go find Cliff and a moment later Wesley was tugging at his hand. He swung his little brother down the steps off the back porch while Paul hurried ahead of them.

"Look. Look at the swing, Cliff," Paul called. He ran on thin little legs and sat down in the swing suspended from a huge oak limb overhead. "Will you swing me?"

"Let's go out to the barn first," he said. "We'll look around and see what's going on out there. Then I'll swing you."

He led them through the gate into the barnyard where his quick eyes scanned the scene. He drew another breath of satisfaction. Everything was just the way he remembered it: the garden on the left and, behind this, the small chicken yard opening from a chicken house; directly across the lot in front of him, the big barn with sweet-smelling hay in the loft and a wide breezy hallway separating the empty mule stalls and small rooms for feed and gear. There was the pigpen on the right side of the lot, a gate that opened out into the fields east of the house, and a large equipment shelter where a man was kneeling beside a tractor to which was attached a strange-looking piece of equipment.

"Come on," Cliff said to the boys. "Let's see what he's doing."

They ran across the lot and stopped beside the man who looked up at them. His broad, handsome face was golden brown and when he laughed his black eyes seemed to sparkle with little lights.

"Good afternoon," he said. His voice was deep and mellow.

"Hi," said Cliff. "My name is Cliff and this is Paul and Wesley. My mama said your name is Hoke Harris."

"That's right," the man said. "It's good to see you boys got here."

"What's that you're working on?" Paul asked.

"This?" Hoke said. He stood up. He was a tall man with broad shoulders and narrow hips. "This is a poisoning machine. Helps to get rid of Old Man Boll Weevil."

"Who's he?" Paul asked. His black eyes were big in his small face.

Hoke broke into a big laugh that rang out across the lot. "You don't know much about farming, do you?"

"We can learn," said Cliff with some dignity.

Hoke looked down at Cliff. His laughter faded to a smile that was gentle and friendly. "That's right, too. And I'll tell you everything I know. I'll show you how to plow, how to chop, and how we spray the cotton with this stuff that kills the boll weevil. They're little insects that eat cotton while it's still in the boll, Paul. If we don't get rid of them we don't have any cotton to sell and that's bad." He adjusted a screw on the machine and moved around to look at a part on the other side. "This is a new machine. The poison comes out these little nozzles and a fan blows it out over the cotton. That makes a fine mist that settles down on the leaves and under them so it can get to the bolls. This new way surely beats the old way we used to do it."

"How was that?" Cliff asked.

"Well, of course, some people with big farms still use airplanes that fly low over the fields and spray the poison out, but you can't always use them and this way really gets the poison down on the cotton better. A long time ago we swabbed poison on with a stick wrapped in burlap and dipped in a mixture of molasses and poison. It took a man a long time to get over an acre of cotton. Now, one man on a tractor with this sprayer can get over a hundred acres in a day."

"Gosh," said Cliff. "That does make farming easier." He bent to see how the machine was attached to the tractor.

"This is about the biggest job we have to do right now until the wheat is ready to harvest," said Hoke.

Paul put out his hand to touch the machine.

"Better not put your hands on it, Paul. You boys will have to be careful about handling things out here because of the poison. So don't play out here around the machinery unless I'm here—or your daddy."

Cliff stepped back and it was then that he saw the boy who had come in through the gate beside the house.

It was a boy about his own height. He was slim and sinewy and blond and he moved toward them with lithe grace. He had the bluest eyes that Cliff had ever seen and a shock of curly blond hair that tumbled over the sun-browned skin of his brow.

All this Cliff saw in an instant and he braced himself for an encounter with a white boy as he always did at school until he knew what attitude he would meet. But his caution was mixed with excitement for behind the boy was a pony, a black and white pony, who breathed heavily as if he had been running and who pawed at the ground as if impatient to be off again.

"Hi," said the boy. "My name's Ted."

Cliff tore his eyes from the pony and looked at the boy again. "Hi," he said. His manner was still cautious and cool.

"I heard you were coming here to live," said Ted. He looked straight at Cliff. His mouth lifted a little to one side in an engaging way when he smiled and his eyes had a merry warmth. His slender face had a slight indentation that appeared to be a small scar beside the mouth.

"Yes," said Cliff. "I guess so."

"I'm glad," said Ted. "There are not any boys my age living very close around here."

Cliff's tension eased a little and he moved to one side to get a better look at the pony. "Is that your pony?"

"Not really mine," said Ted. "He belongs to my granddaddy, but he lets me claim him. I'm just staying with him this summer. I live in Raleigh."

"Oh," said Cliff. "I used to live there."

"Did you really?" Ted said. "Is this the first time you've lived on a farm?"

Caution crept back into Cliff's manner. He did not want to admit he was new to farm life. Not to this white boy.

"Oh, I used to visit here," he said casually. Then he changed the subject back to the pony which filled his mind. "Do you get to ride him every day?" he asked.

"Oh, sure. I ride him all the time whenever I'm not helping my grandfather. You want to ride him?" His eyes when he looked at Cliff were direct and open with warm friendliness.

Cliff ached to get on the pony but he had never been on one and he was not sure he could ride. He did not want to seem awkward in front of this boy.

"I don't know," he said. "It's getting sort of late." He reached out and touched the pony's neck. The hair was smooth and damp and a warm sweet odor rose from his flesh.

"Well, it is almost suppertime and I promised Grandma I'd come straight back home," Ted said. "But I could come back tomorrow."

"Okay," said Cliff, disappointed and relieved at the same time. "That'll be fine."

He watched Ted jump lightly onto the pony's back throwing one leg over easily and adjusting himself quickly. Ted flicked the reins and the pony responded immediately, trotting off, his beautiful thick tail flowing behind him. Cliff watched him go with envy filling his mind. Some people had all the luck, he thought.

"Why didn't you ride him, Cliff?" Paul asked as they walked toward the house. "That's all you've talked about lately."

"Oh, be quiet, Paul," he said. "You know I promised to swing you before supper."

5

CRICKET

Cliff awoke the next morning to find Mama standing beside the bed shaking him gently.

"Time to get up, Cliff. Daddy left a lot of things for you to do and you need to find out about some of them."

"Yes, ma'am," Cliff said, springing out of bed and looking through the window where the sun was already flooding the fields with golden light. Ted would be coming back with the pony this morning. Maybe he was already on his way.

"I have breakfast almost ready. You'll have to stir earlier here on the farm than you did in the city."

Cliff slipped into his clothes and walked barefooted onto the pleasant back porch where Mama was just pouring coffee into her green coffee cup. Paul and Wesley were already at the table eating cereal. Cliff touched Wesley's head lightly and said "Hi" to Paul who threw up his hand between bites. He could hear the busy chatter of birds in the trees that had limbs growing down over the roof of the porch. The morning was cool and breakfast looked good.

Cliff drank his orange juice and helped his plate to the eggs, then took one of the light fluffy biscuits.

"I thought Daddy would stay around for a few days," Cliff said.

"No, he had to get out early this morning. He is trying to sell his assigned quota before he gives up his work with the company. He may be able to come home some nights but he wants to leave with a good record so he can go back with them if this farming doesn't work out."

Cliff looked at her in quick alarm. "You mean we might not stay down here?" His heart almost sank with the thought.

"Well, of course, Daddy wants to stay. But Uncle Ed had not quite finished paying for the farm and we'll have to pay that if we decide to stay here."

"I didn't realize that Daddy had to pay anything."

"The house is already paid for," said Mama. "He is just taking up the payments that were still due on the farm. The land is worth a lot and more than half of that is already paid for. It's just hard because we didn't have much extra money set aside that we could use to pay for it. But if the next two or three years are good farm years, and if we watch our pennies, things may work out so we can stay here and Daddy can work the farm without having to worry about any extra job."

Cliff thought a long time. "Wouldn't it help if Daddy kept his job now and let Hoke run the farm?"

"Hoke says he will not be able to help us long because of some other work he has to do. I'm afraid we can't depend on him."

"Maybe Daddy could find somebody else."

"It isn't easy to find someone who will look after your property the way you would," said Mama. "Some people are not as careful about other people's property as they should be." She wiped Wesley's mouth and helped him down from his chair. "You know that I don't like for us to borrow things, but when we do we have to cherish them as if they were our own. Not everybody feels that way."

Cliff thought about that—about how much he would cherish the pony if he won it. He realized as he thought of this that his hope for winning the pony was beginning to fade. It had been three weeks, now, since the contest ended.

He heard the sound of a motor outside and looked at Mama. "That must be Hoke's car. He may need me to help him."

"Daddy said he wanted you to help Hoke with the chickens and the garden, and the roof on the barn needs some patching. Hoke will show you," Mama said.

"You want to go?" Cliff asked Paul who nodded and slipped out of his chair. But Mama spoke.

"Stay here and play with Wesley in the swing, Paul, until I get through the dishes. Then I can take him in here with me."

Cliff ran out to join Hoke who was already in the feed room of the barn.

"Hi," said Cliff as he stepped up into the little room that smelled of crushed corn and dry oats.

"Good morning," said Hoke, his quick smile lighting his face. "So you're going to be my working partner. Ready to get started?"

"Yes, sir," said Cliff. "What do we start off doing?"

Hoke handed him a bucket and filled it full of cracked grain.

"This has a lot of stuff mixed in with it to make the chickens grow fast. Your Uncle Ed always raised good chickens."

It seemed to Cliff that Uncle Ed must have done everything pretty well. He had certainly made lots of money to build such a nice house and pay for half of the good farm.

"Did he sell chickens, too?" Cliff asked.

"Oh, he sold most of the roosters. Kept the hens for laying and a few for frying as he needed them. He sold right many eggs, too," Hoke said. "Yes, sir. A chicken is a valuable creature. Hey, you know a chicken and a hog were talking one day about the difference in their value. How do you think they came out?"

"Do you mean which is worth most?"

"No, which gives more to mankind."

"Well, the hog's the biggest," said Cliff.

"The hog and the chicken were eating eggs and bacon for breakfast. The hog said to the hen, 'The hen that gave these eggs made a donation to this breakfast, but the hog made a sacrifice.'"

It took a moment for Cliff to think about that and

then he laughed. "Yeah, that was a sacrifice," he said, laughing again, his bright face lighting with humor and fun. "I guess the hog does give most to mankind."

Hoke laughed a big free laugh that brought more laughter to Cliff's lips.

He watched Hoke's jaunty strides as they crossed the barn lot to the chicken yard and heard the catchy tune Hoke whistled. It made doing the chores seem a merry activity. They went into the chicken house where the flock of chickens crowded about them. They walked over Cliff's feet and pecked at his shoes. Hoke showed Cliff how to open the empty automatic chicken feeders and put feed in so that the grain would sift down into the troughs as the chickens ate. This way, there was always a tray full of feed. Yet, the chickens could not turn the troughs over and spill the feed on the ground.

The watering troughs were constructed much the same way. Huge containers of water turned upside down onto the trays allowed a small amount of water to flow into them as the chickens drank it down to a certain level.

Cliff helped Hoke fill the jars with water from the water spigot in the lot and then they fed the old sow. She was penned up inside a fence on the right side of the barn. Cliff watched the ten little pigs hunt hungrily around their mother while she ate from the automatic feeder that he and Hoke filled from outside the fence. He laughed when they settled down to real nursing after she had finished eating and had lain down so they could find their places.

"The littlest one can't find a place," he said.

"It's first come, first served around here," Hoke said cheerfully and Cliff laughed. "If he's not man enough to get a better place I guess that's just his tough luck."

"I'll help him," Cliff said, starting to climb over the fence.

"Better stay out of that pen, Cliff. The old sow can eat you alive if she thinks you're after her pigs."

Cliff stopped midway over the fence thinking how many ways there were to get into trouble on a farm. Activities here could be as dangerous as in the railroad yards if you didn't know how to look after yourself.

It was then that he saw Ted coming up the dirt road from the main highway.

"Oh, gosh," he said. "There's Ted. He's going to let me ride his pony. Is there anything else to do? Do you think I could stop and ride a while?"

"Nothing to do that can't wait until tomorrow, Cliff. Your daddy wanted us to work on the barn roof where it's leaking a little, but I've got to go to town and get some more poison so we can spray the cotton again. So you go ahead. I'll see you later."

Ted rode into the yard and Cliff opened the barnyard gate so that he could come through. Once inside, Ted slid quickly off the pony's back.

"What's his name?" Cliff asked.

"I just call him Cricket," said Ted.

"Cricket," Cliff repeated. The name seemed to fit. He walked around to view the pony from the other side.

"Hey, don't walk so close behind him!" Ted said sharply. Cliff jumped aside quickly, frightened.

"Don't you know anything about ponies?"

Cliff bristled with resentment and he looked sidelong at Ted, expecting scorn, but the boy's bright blue eyes smiled straight back at him.

"Sometimes a pony kicks when you get too close to his

heels." Ted's expression held no trace of bossiness or criticism.

"He's being honest with me," Cliff thought. "He really wants to be friendly and I've got to be on the level with him. I can't pretend."

"Have you ever ridden a pony before?" Ted asked.

Cliff shook his head. "I've hardly ever seen a real one," he said. "Much less ridden one."

"Okay," said Ted. "You're in the same fix I was in the first time I came down here to see Granddaddy. I thought I'd never learn to stay on a pony."

Cliff felt a degree of relief. He was glad he had told Ted the truth. Now he didn't have to worry if he didn't do so well.

"Don't you need a saddle when you're learning to ride?" he asked.

"Granddaddy said it was better to learn to ride bareback. That way, if you fall off, your foot can't get caught in a stirrup and the pony won't drag you around."

"Oh, I see," Cliff said.

"It may be harder to stay on right at first," Ted said, "but I like to ride this way best. You feel sort of like you are a part of the pony."

Cliff nodded.

Ted looked around the lot. "This is a good place to learn because Cricket can't get out and he doesn't have a chance to build up much speed before he gets from one fence to the other. If we can just put a board across the end of that shelter so he won't run under there where the farm implements are."

They found a long plank under the barn and braced it across the tractor shelter.

Then Ted said, "Okay, Cliff. Try it."

Cliff drew a deep breath and walked up to Cricket's right side.

"No," yelled Ted. "Don't ever get up on that side. Come around to the left side."

"Why is that?" Cliff asked.

"I don't know. That's just the way everybody does it," Ted said.

Cliff gave Cricket's rear end plenty of margin as he walked around to the other side.

"You've got to jump up on him," Ted said, "so your stomach is across his back. Then you throw your leg over. Like this. Look."

Ted caught the reins in his left hand and then gave a big spring which tossed him so that he lay on his stomach halfway across the pony's back. In a flash his right leg was over the pony's back and he pulled himself up erect. With a quick jerk of the reins and a light kick in the ribs, Ted spurred Cricket to a canter. At the end of the lot next to the garden he pulled Cricket to a halt, turned shortly, and cantered back.

Cliff watched with a measure of envy. It looked so easy.

6

RIDING LESSON

The two boys looked at the pony who stood patiently as time hung motionless in the sun-washed barnyard. Somewhere in the distance a dog was barking and the lonely sound of it pierced the quietness of the moment, but Cliff could hear only the rapid beating of his heart. Here, finally, was the moment he must begin to ride a pony. He had to get on Cricket. Right now. This minute.

"Go ahead. Try it," Ted urged.

Cliff took a deep breath, held the reins in his left hand and crouched a bit, then gave a spring. It was not nearly hard enough. The pony lurched and jerked away as Cliff fell against his side.

"Harder," said Ted. "You've got to jump higher."

Cliff tried again. This time he almost made it but the pony moved off before he could get himself up quite far enough to throw his leg over. He felt himself sliding off before he could push himself over.

"Hey, wait," Ted called. "Let me help you on the first time."

"I can do it," Cliff said stubbornly. "Let me try again."

For the third time he tried. This time he jumped so hard that the upper part of his body went too far over. He was sliding off headfirst on the other side. He dropped the reins and hit the ground beside the pony, breaking the fall with his hands.

Ted doubled up with laughter and Cliff sat up, laughing, too. For a moment he sat there and they laughed together. Then Ted spoke.

"I bet you make it next time. You've jumped too hard, and you've jumped too easy. You've got to jump somewhere in between."

Cliff got to his feet. His shoulder ached from the fall. He grasped the reins and the pony's mane in his left hand and then jumped lightly from the balls of his feet as he thrust himself up and forward. He sprawled across the pony's back, feeling the ridge of Cricket's backbone directly under the middle of his stomach. The pony moved off but Cliff tightened his grasp on the thick mane and held on while he kicked and struggled to get his right leg over the pony's back. Now, it was over. His legs hung down on each of the pony's sides. He pulled himself to a sitting position, still clutching the mane tightly. Cricket moved slowly but Cliff felt himself slipping from one side to the other with the pony's movements.

"I can't stay on," he said more to himself than to Ted.

"Clamp your legs close to his sides," Ted called.

Cliff tightened his legs against the pony's smooth sides and Cricket, mistaking it for a signal to trot, began to run. His backbone hit against Cliff's bottom with solid blows. The wind seemed to rush past Cliff's face. He felt as if they were flying. He bounced and jounced on the pony's back and he held on to the mane for dear life.

"Make him go faster so he won't bounce you so bad." Ted's words fell on his jarred ears.

"W-what do you mean—faster? This is fast enough for me," Cliff tried to call back, but his teeth clattered together so he could not get the words out. He was sure that Cricket was setting some kind of speed record.

"You need to gallop," Ted shouted. "That rides easier."

"I need to walk first," Cliff tried to shout back but his words were lost in his throat as the pony trotted on.

They came to the end of the lot next to the garden. The pony wheeled and turned sharply and Cliff felt himself slipping. He tried to pull himself erect but his shoulders seemed to go one way and his hips another. Cricket started cantering back toward Ted, and Cliff could no longer hold the mane. His fingers were slipping.

"I can't hold on," he yelled and then he slipped off completely, landing with a sharp thud against the ground, his head snapping back with a stunning blow.

For a moment he lay quite still, his hip throbbing painfully, and then he saw Ted bending over him anxiously.

"You all right?" he asked.

"Yep. I'm all right," said Cliff. He rolled over and got up, wincing only slightly at the pain he felt in his hip and leg. He brushed himself off. "Maybe I'll do better next time."

Ted looked at him with admiration. "Let's get on him together," he said. "That'll help until you can get used to the way it feels to be on a pony."

Ted leaped onto Cricket's back and then rode him up beside the old sow's pen. Cliff, who waited on the top plank of the fence, threw his sore leg over Cricket's back and slipped on behind Ted, wrapping his arms tightly about Ted's waist. Together they rode around and around the lot.

Cliff began to grow accustomed to the feel of the pony's flesh and muscles beneath his legs. He began to feel the rhythm of the pony's movement, to know the degree of pressure he needed to exert with his legs in order to hold himself steady on Cricket's back. When he finally tried again to ride alone he found it easier and easier to stay erect and to ride without holding on to the mane.

"That's good," Ted said when he had cantered about the lot for the sixteenth time. "That's real good. I think you could go almost anywhere now."

"It's really fun," Cliff said. "I just wish I had one so we could ride together."

"Maybe your daddy will get you one sometime. Granddaddy has right many to sell."

Cliff thought of how Mama had told him this morning they must be careful with the pennies and he rejected the idea. He could not possibly ask Daddy to buy a pony now. He went back to his old dream of winning the pony. It really was his only chance but, somehow, his hope was not so bright. Suddenly, he wanted to tell Ted all about his effort to win the pony. Ted had a way of listening so that everything you said seemed to be important.

"I entered a contest last winter and I thought I might

win the pony they were giving as a prize," he said. "But I haven't heard anything from them. I'm afraid I might not have won it."

He realized as he said the words that this was the very first time he had been able to admit the possibility that he really might not win the pony. Mama had been trying to get him to face this fact all summer, but he had not wanted to. Now, suddenly, here with this boy, he wanted to be strictly honest. He knew he should have heard about the pony if he had won. They sat together under the shade of the oaks at the edge of the barn lot next to the yard while Cliff told Ted about the contest and how he had sold the seed and entered his name for the final drawing.

"I wrote to them before we left to come here," Cliff said, "but I haven't heard a word so I'm pretty sure I didn't win."

"Gee, that's really tough," said Ted, "after all that work you did—selling the seed and all." A tiny frown had appeared between his blue eyes and his quick sensitive mouth widened with an expression of sympathy. Somehow, his attitude was comforting.

"I've still got the four dollars," said Cliff. "But I guess that's not enough to even buy feed for a pony for a week, much less paying for one."

"Granddaddy said it didn't cost so much to feed a pony if you had good grazing for him," said Ted. "I wanted to buy one, too. But living in the city all you can do is wish."

"I know," said Cliff.

"That's one reason why my folks let me come down to spend the summer with Granddaddy. This is the first time

I've stayed all summer. I used to come just for a few days at the time."

"I guess that's why I didn't get to see you when I came to see Uncle Ed that time."

"Gosh, I sure wish I could stay down here all the time," Ted said.

"And I wish I had all the ponies you have to ride," said Cliff.

They looked at each other and laughed. Cliff felt a strange and delightful sense that his thoughts and feelings were extended into another person, making them double fun. The moment seemed rich with friendliness and re- laxed pleasure.

"Granddaddy doesn't have many ponies that you can ride. Most of them aren't broken to ride. He raises them to sell," said Ted after a time. "He's taking some to a sale pretty soon."

"Where does he sell them?" Cliff asked.

"He takes some to Goldsboro and some to Suffolk, Virginia, now and then. But most of them he sells here on the farm."

They looked up as Paul came out to join them and when he asked to ride, they helped him on the pony. Cliff held him on while Ted led the pony about the barn- yard, holding him by the bridle. Once or twice Mama came out into the barnyard and watched them as they helped Paul and took turns riding themselves. Once she even let Wesley ride with Ted. Wesley sat up in front of Ted who held him tight with one hand, the reins in the other.

Time slipped by so quickly that Cliff could hardly be- lieve how late it was when Ted said he had promised his grandmother that he would be back by twelve.

It was a little after twelve when Cliff checked on the time. Ted jumped on the pony while Cliff opened the gate for him to go through the yard.

"If you want to ride with me around the Neck, I'll come for you in the morning and we'll go together," Ted said. His left hand, holding the reins, rested lightly on Cricket's mane.

"I'll be ready," Cliff told Ted happily. Ted gave the pony a light touch of the reins. Cricket was off in a fast canter and Cliff watched the tiny puffs of dust that rose where his flying feet touched the path.

"Come in the house, Cliff," Mama called. There was urgency in her voice.

Cliff was suddenly aware of his body. His muscles felt sore and stiff. His hip and shoulder were sore. He found that his legs were weak and shaky and he looked down to see if they were really bowed out like ice tongs or if they only felt that way. He walked stiffly up the steps onto the back porch.

"Cliff," his mother said. "Paul just came back from the mail box. The mailman left a letter for you. It's in

"Cliff," his mother said. "Paul just came back from the seed company."

Cliff stared at her, hardly believing what he heard. A letter from the seed company. Could it be that he had won the pony, after all? Just when he had given up hope? Were they writing to tell him he had won the pony? He almost stumbled in his haste to get to the living room where the letter waited for him.

7

DAY OF GLOOM

The room seemed to be bursting with silence as Cliff folded the letter, slipped it back inside the envelope and laid it on the desk. Even though he had admitted to Ted that he might not win the pony, to see the actual words that he was not the winner written in black and white was a terrible blow. His body, already stiff and sore from his morning on the pony, felt suddenly weak and there was an aching hollow in the middle of his stomach just below his ribs.

When Mama called him to lunch he could only nibble at the food. Her words of comfort made him want to cry and he had to fight to keep back the tears. All afternoon he wandered about the house doing things that Mama asked him to do, automatically, hardly knowing what he was doing. He put away linen and helped to store Wesley's clothes in the big chest of drawers that the two little boys would share. He helped unpack some of the boxes of china that he had packed up before they left the city. And he looked after Wesley while Mama fixed supper for them, rescuing Paul when the boys had a fight.

"He hit me," Paul complained to Cliff.

"Did you hit Paul on purpose, Wesley?" Cliff asked.

"What's on purpose?" Wesley asked.

"It means—" Cliff started to answer.

"I know what it means," said Paul. He was rubbing his skinny arm where the blow had landed.

"What?" Wesley asked. "What does it mean?" He was banging the side of a tree with a toy shovel.

"It means . . . Let's see." Paul searched for a definition. "It means you might get a spanking."

"Ah, you guys, quit it," said Cliff wearily. "Let's go in and wash up. We can sit on the front porch."

The sounds of the evening came softly across the fields to Cliff as he waited on the porch for his brothers who were in the bathroom squabbling good-naturedly over who would use the soap first.

Above their noise he could hear the birds chirping in quiet little tones as they prepared for the night. The wind rustled ever so slightly through the trees. Far overhead the raucous chant of a July fly cut through the evening air as if it were mocking Cliff.

"Aw, hush your fuss," Cliff said. He longed to walk

out into the woods behind the house and throw himself on the ground and howl. He wished he could see Ted and tell him about it. He knew that Ted, probably better than anyone else, would know exactly how he felt.

Later in the evening when he went to bed, no tears came. He lay on his back, staring into the darkness, his body aching and the words of the letter appearing before his eyes.

"We are sorry," the letter had said, "to inform you that you were not one of the winners in our recent contest. We appreciate your interest in our product and in the effort you put forth in sales. We hope that you will continue to find our seed satisfactory." They had enclosed a list of the lucky people and Cliff could only think with envy of the lady from Winston-Salem who had won the pony.

"She probably weighs two hundred and ninety pounds and lives on a crowded street," he thought dismally.

He slept finally, but he was restless and when he awoke with the morning sun in his face he did not bounce out of bed with his usual liveliness. His legs were stiff and his hip ached, but these were minor in comparison with the heaviness he felt inside. There was just nothing to which he could look forward. It was going to be hard to like everything here on the farm without being able to even hope for a pony. Maybe he could save enough, somehow, to buy one like Ted said. He thought of the four dollars. That might be a start. Maybe Daddy would put him on an allowance. He wanted to see Ted and he wanted to have a look at Mr. Taylor's ponies. He needed to find out how much they cost.

He could hear Hoke out in the barnyard. He was singing in a deep mellow voice:

"All my girls are daffy
Crazy over me
But none can touch Miss Jenny
'Cause she's my honeybee."

Mama came in and got him out of bed. She hustled him through breakfast so he could go out to help Hoke.

"You can help him hoe the garden this morning. And I want you to help me pick the string beans late this afternoon when it gets cooler. The weatherman says we'll have showers today and tonight, and I want to get the beans in the freezer before they get too old."

"But Ted said he was coming up to ride around the farm," Cliff said.

"You can ride a little while if he comes," said Mama. "But there are lots of things to be done and we need you to help."

Cliff helped Hoke feed up and then Hoke showed him how to hoe the fall garden which had been planted to produce a second crop of vegetables.

The vegetables planted in the spring were already heavy with their harvest. The tomato vines were ladened with fine ripe tomatoes. Cabbages almost as large as footballs stretched down two long rows. Butter beans and string beans hung from the vines. Beets, carrots, and radishes were bursting from the earth, and squash and cucumbers lay hidden among the vines.

When Hoke was satisfied that Cliff could work carefully around the tiny green plants that were just coming up, he picked up his own hoe and prepared to leave. "I've got a little work to do up at my house," he said. "I'm going to take the sprayer up there so if I get through I can finish spraying that cotton field there by my house.

Your daddy wants the roof on the barn patched where it's leaking and I had hoped we could get to that this afternoon before it rains again, but I'm not sure there will be time."

Cliff chopped up weeds and pulled out grass, trying not to think about his stiff sore limbs and the pony he had not won. But he kept looking down the lane next to the woods, hoping to see Ted come up on Cricket. It was hot in the garden and he longed to see Ted for more than one reason. He wanted to tell him about the pony and he wanted to get out of the garden for a little while.

Mama came out to see how he was getting along as the morning wore on.

"Where's Hoke?" she asked.

"He said he had some work to do and he was going to spray the cotton if he got through."

"I thought he was going to stay here and get the garden worked out," she said. "It really looks too much like rain to do the spraying today and I know Daddy was anxious to get the barn fixed."

She looked at the beans. "They're ready right now to go into the freezer. No need to let them go to waste. We'll just have to get them this afternoon."

Cliff felt another downward surge of spirits. She meant business. She was going to make him pick the beans. "I'm still looking for Ted," he said.

"Well, it's eleven o'clock already and he's probably not coming this morning," Mama said.

"He said he was coming." Cliff set his lips together stubbornly.

"Well, there's plenty to do here. It's really not a very good time for you to go off riding a pony. You'll have time to do a lot of that later. I'm sure it's better for you to keep busy—today especially. So you keep on working on the garden." She looked out across the field beyond the garden toward Hoke's home. "I don't understand why Hoke left."

She went back into the house and the rest of the morning Cliff chopped and hoped, but at lunchtime when Ted had not shown up, he threw his hoe down and went into the house in utter dejection. He still did not have much appetite for the fresh vegetables that Mama had prepared for them.

"Have you finished the garden?" Mama asked him.

"I don't think you ever get through working a garden," said Cliff gloomily. "Looks like to me the weeds grow behind you as fast as you chop."

Mama laughed. "I guess everything looks a little wrong to you today, Cliff. That's not hard to understand when you've had such a disappointment, but you keep at it. Daddy's depending on you."

Cliff scowled a little. It wasn't much fun working out there in the hot sunshine all by yourself—disappointment or no disappointment.

After lunch, Mama and the boys lay down to take a nap and Cliff went back to the garden. It had grown hotter and the rows stretched endlessly, it seemed. Cliff chopped and grumbled. Hoke was gone. Mama was asleep. Paul and Wesley were lying in the cool house. Nobody working but Cliff. He went to the house twice for water. Everything there was quiet.

Back in the garden he kept wishing Ted would come just so he could get away from this job for a little while. Mama said he could ride if Ted came. Maybe she wouldn't mind if he stopped a little while and ran up to see what was keeping Ted. Maybe he could find out how much Mr.

Taylor would charge for a pony. He wondered again why Ted had not come as he had promised. The thought occurred to him that maybe Mr. Taylor did not want Ted to play with a Negro boy, but Cliff put the idea aside. Ted would not have come the first day if this were true and, besides, Ted was so friendly, he was certain this was not it. He looked at the house. Everything was quiet. It wouldn't take long to walk the mile to Mr. Taylor's. He'd be back before Mama and the boys got up from their nap.

Sudden resolution filled him and he put down his hoe.

8

BLACK CLOUDS GATHERING

Away from the house his spirits began to rise a bit as he thought of seeing Ted and Cricket, of visiting the farm where so many ponies roamed over the pasture. He walked along the path close to the woods, stopping now and then to look at something that interested him.

He passed Hoke's neat little house where Hoke lived alone and he wondered how much of the cotton Hoke had sprayed. The sprayer was still sitting beside the house and Hoke's car was just in front of it but there was no sign of Hoke. "He must be eating his lunch, too," Cliff thought. "Or maybe he's taking a nap like everybody else."

Cliff met a rabbit and they stared at each other face to

face before the rabbit hopped slowly out into a field of peanuts and then around Cliff to reach the woods.

"You crazy rabbit," Cliff said. "Why did you go all around me to get to the woods. If I had been a hunter, I'd have shot you for sure."

He found a Venus's-flytrap in the same place Uncle Ed had pointed them out along the edge of the woods and he lay on his stomach for a time, inserting a tiny weed between the two serrated pods that snapped shut as he touched them. He thought with wonder how strange it was that a plant could attract an insect and then capture it within its grasp like some terrible monster. He walked on past little paths that led into the woods, wondering where they all went and he looked overhead at the darkening clouds as they scudded across the face of the sun.

It was close to two o'clock when he came to the first pasture and saw the ponies. There were black ones and gray ones and red ones with white manes and tails. They looked up curiously as Cliff passed them.

He whistled softly. They began to run toward him and, as he walked south toward the house and barns, they followed him on the other side of the fence. He stopped now and then to rub a nose or to pat the long smooth neck of one of them. He laughed at the little colts that kicked up their heels and scampered in big loops about the pasture, then came back to walk saucily along beside their mothers. A beautiful red stallion with a sweeping white mane and tail nickered and stamped about his mares between his charges up to the fence to have a look at Cliff.

Cliff saw Ted in the big barnyard with his grandfather who was working with some of the ponies. He hesitated. They might not want him around. Ted might not be friendly today. Some white boys were like that—friendly one day and cold the next. Cliff approached cautiously.

They looked up as Cliff drew near them and Ted's face brightened.

"Hello, Cliff," he said.

"Hi," said Cliff.

"Granddaddy," said Ted turning toward the man. "This is Cliff Morgan."

Mr. Taylor stopped what he was doing and looked up at Cliff. He nodded. "How are you, young man?" He was a big man. He had a long ruddy face and graying hair. His eyes were blue, like Ted's, and they crinkled at the corners when he smiled at Cliff.

"I'm fine," Cliff said. He breathed more easily, happy that they seemed so friendly, not thinking now of his limbs which had been so sore all day or of the heat which had bothered him in the garden.

"I couldn't get back up there this morning," Ted said. "We're getting the ponies ready for the sale in August."

"Yep," said Mr. Taylor. "Lots to do before a sale." He was trimming a pony's foot, holding it firmly between his knees while Ted held the pony's nose with a rope that was twisted about the pony's upper lip.

"Hear you've moved in and will be my neighbor," said Mr. Taylor.

"Yes, sir. That's right," said Cliff.

"Think you'll like being a farm boy?"

"Oh, yes, sir. I like it already. I visited Uncle Ed one year and I could hardly wait to get back down here again. It's hard to realize I'll be living here all the time now."

Mr. Taylor did not look up, but kept working on the pony's foot.

"Know anything about ponies?"

"Not much, except what Ted has told me," said Cliff. "I'd like to though. I'd like to know everything there is to know about them."

"Well, now. That's a big order and if you depend on Ted for all your knowledge, you'll be a long time learning," said Mr. Taylor.

Ted giggled in the way that made Cliff feel like laughing, too.

"He's been working with them all summer, though," continued Mr. Taylor, "and he's coming along."

"Doesn't that hurt the pony?" Cliff asked, edging around to watch more closely as Mr. Taylor cut out the center of the hoof he was trimming.

"No more than cutting your fingernails."

"How about his lip?" he asked looking at the rope twisted about the pony's upper lip. "Isn't Ted hurting his lip?"

"Not as long as he stands still. That's the way you keep a pony quiet to work on him when you have to do something that requires them to be still. I'm trying to get them shined up for selling. Got a few more than I like to keep. Have to weed out a few every year. Usually, I get rid of those I don't care about keeping."

Cliff looked at the beautiful sorrel pony, his red coat gleaming. The pony looked perfect to Cliff.

"What's the matter with this one?" he asked.

"Well, the biggest thing is that he's not registered and I'm trying to get my unregistered stock weeded out."

He explained to Cliff that registered stock were ponies which were descended from strong parent lines whose sires and dams had papers showing they were from good stock. He told Cliff about the difference in the cost of ponies, pointing out that a registered pony might sell for a thousand or even ten thousand dollars while an unregistered pony might sell for one hundred or even fifty dollars. "And it really doesn't cost much more to raise a registered one than an unregistered one," he said.

Cliff thought of his four dollars and he sighed.

"I'd be satisfied with any kind," he said.

Mr. Taylor let Cliff comb one down for him with the curry comb, getting tangles out of the mane and tail. Then Cliff brushed the hair until it was smooth and shining. He and Ted walked some of the ponies about the lot as though showing them in a ring and they rode some of them with a saddle. Ted showed Cliff how to post. Cliff pressed the balls of his feet against the stirrups and lifted himself from the saddle with every alternating rise of the pony's back as he trotted. It was fun, but like Ted, Cliff preferred riding bareback.

Mr. Taylor showed Cliff how to harness a pony to his cart and then allowed Cliff to unharness him by himself.

"You've got a real knack with ponies, Cliff," Mr. Taylor told him, and Cliff beamed with pride. Ted, who was working on another at the same time, grinned, too.

"He's a pretty good pony student," Ted said.

He watched while Mr. Taylor trimmed some of the ponies with shears and was so absorbed that he did not notice that time was passing swiftly or that the sun was now completely hidden behind dark clouds.

"I don't have but a few that can be ridden," said Mr. Taylor when Cliff asked about breaking the ponies. "It really would be good to have somebody who could break a few for me from time to time. I have people who come down here and ask for broke ponies every now and then."

"I'd be glad to help you, anytime," said Cliff.

Ted laughed again. "He's already had some experience in how to fall off a pony," he said.

Mr. Taylor looked at Cliff and smiled. "That goes with learning how," he said. "They say you have to fall off a pony at least three times before you really learn to ride."

"Cliff, you've only got one time to go," said Ted.

"How about you?" Cliff asked.

"I've learned how about four times at that rate," said Ted giggling again.

"I think that raising ponies would be the nicest job in the whole wide world," said Cliff.

"Well there are a few problems," said Mr. Taylor. "They get out occasionally and this is bad if the stallions get together and fight. But there is really not much way you can go wrong with a pony. They can live indefinitely on grass but, of course, they need a little grain and supplement to keep their coats glossy and their spirit high. I mix in a few vitamins and give them salt to lick, and they get a little something to control worms. About the only thing you can do to get in real trouble is to feed them the wrong thing."

"The wrong thing?" Cliff asked.

"Yep. That's right. You have to be careful that what they eat is not spoiled. If they eat molded grain or wet peanut vines they can get mighty sick. If they graze in a rye patch that has headed out just before they foal, they'll lose their colts."

"Lose their colts?"

"That's right. The little foals will die. They come too soon before they're strong enough to nurse or even to stand up, sometimes. Of course, they can't live that way. It's hard to save a foal when he can't nurse his mother."

"Gosh," said Cliff. "There really is a lot to know about raising ponies."

"Not much if you take it a little at a time. It's really about the easiest animal to care for as long as you're careful not to feed too much or even a little of the wrong thing."

Time had passed so quickly that it was almost dark before Cliff realized it and Mrs. Taylor was calling Mr. Taylor and Ted to come in.

"Oh, I didn't know it was so late. Mama will be mad as hops when I get home," he said thinking for the first time of the beans he was supposed to pick and the barn roof that Hoke said they might work on.

"I'll take you home," said Ted.

"Looks like a bad cloud over there," said Mr. Taylor, nodding toward a heavy fast-moving cloud that had long rain streaks falling from it in the west. Cliff saw this for the first time.

"Why don't you just ride one of the ponies home, Cliff?" Mr. Taylor said.

Cliff gasped. "You mean me—ride him home by myself?"

"Sure. You can keep him until tomorrow and bring him back when you have time."

"Oh, no, sir. I couldn't do that."

"Why not?" Mr. Taylor asked. "You might even keep him a few days and get him in good shape for the sale. I've got more than I can handle and I'd be glad for you to work on one of them. Wouldn't you like that?"

"Oh, boy. Would I?" Cliff said. "I'd like it more than anything I can think of, but I don't know what Daddy and Mama would say."

"Just tell them Mr. Taylor said it would be an accommodation to him to have you help with the pony."

"Well, if you put it that way, maybe they wouldn't mind," said Cliff. His heart was beating fast with excitement but he had a strange uneasy feeling of doubt, too. Mama didn't like for him to borrow things.

"You've got a good stable, I know, and there's peanut hay in the barn that your Uncle Ed put up last fall after he harvested his peanuts. It won't hurt for you to groom him and ride him for a few days. It will make him easier to handle in the ring. They sell better that way."

"I'll sure be happy to take care of him for you, Mr. Taylor." He'd just forget about Mama.

"Well, let's see," said Mr. Taylor. He walked about the barn lot and picked out a gray pony with a jet black mane and tail.

"This will be a good one. He's broke good and I don't think you'll have any trouble with him. Let's get a bridle on this one, Ted."

"Oh, my," said Cliff, practically speechless, now. "I'll take good care of him. You can bet on that." He kept pushing back the strong sense of doubt.

"His name is Fast Buck," said Ted as they slipped the bit between the pony's teeth and the straps over his ears. "He'll fly if you kick his sides and give him a loose rein."

Cliff mounted him easily, but even as he rode off, leaving Ted who watched him go, Cliff thought: "I'd better take the back road and come up behind the barn. Mama will have a fit if she knows I've got this pony that belongs to Mr. Taylor. And no telling what Daddy will do." He looked overhead and saw that the cloud was upon him.

"Get going, Fast Buck," he said under his breath. "We may be in trouble more ways than one by the time we get home." He gave Fast Buck a quick nudge in the sides. The pony leaped out into the lane in a flying gallop as the black cloud swept toward them.

9

THE STORM BREAKS

He was almost halfway home when the storm came tearing across the fields with clouds of dust and huge drops of rain that lashed his back and stung his ears. He gave Fast Buck another quick kick in the ribs but the pony was already racing along the path as if forty demons were after him. Cliff hung on with his legs clamped tightly against the pony's sides, his eyes squinted against the increasing force of the rain that blew against them from the back and ran down his face. When heavy gusts of rain caught him in their fury he was blinded so that he could hardly see the path ahead of him.

A searing flash of lightning tore across the sky like

jagged teeth and a heavy crash of thunder followed, making Fast Buck leap out with a new burst of speed.

The path was becoming muddy, but Fast Buck sped on. Splashes of mud exploded about them as his feet hit the sheets of water on the path. On and on the pony ran thrusting his body through the wild and driving storm.

The house and barns loomed up before them and Cliff pulled the left rein. No use to follow the path that curved around in front of the house. Better go along the woods beside the corn field and go into the barnyard through the gate from the east fields. No use to take a chance on having Mama see him come home on the pony. Maybe he wouldn't have to tell her.

He circled the barnyard and slid off the pony at the gate. Another sharp streak of lightning split the sky. He unfastened the gate with fumbling fingers while thunder roared overhead. He led Fast Buck across the lot and into the shelter of the barn. The peace and quiet of the dark hallway enveloped him like warm arms. The sweet smell of hay and leather filled his nostrils.

He leaned against the wet pony and felt the heaving sides pulse beneath his arm. For a moment he stood looking out. Flashes of lightning followed by earth-shaking rolls of thunder and sheets of slanted rain made goose bumps rise along his arms and he pressed closer to the pony. It seemed to him that he had never seen a storm so violent. He noticed thin streams of water dripping down inside the barn and remembered that Hoke planned to patch the barn roof.

"He's a little late getting around to it, I guess," he thought. "But I reckon almost any place would leak in this storm."

As the storm subsided and the rolls of thunder began to

move into the distance, Cliff hunted about in the gathering darkness until he found an old burlap bag. He rubbed it gently down Fast Buck's legs, soaking up much of the water. When he had dried the pony as much as possible he led him into one of the large stalls.

"This will be nice and dry for you, Fast Buck. I'll get you some hay and see if there's some corn left in the grain box." He spoke softly, almost in a whisper and then he turned to leave the pony.

Fast Buck shook himself and whinnied, a high squealing sound. Cliff wheeled around and flung himself back against the pony.

"Hush that stuff, Fast Buck," he said. He stroked the pony's neck with quick nervous movements. "Don't make so much noise. My mama may be on the back porch and it's better if she doesn't know you're out here." He looked anxiously toward the house but it was impossible to see through the semidarkness and the rain.

"Now, you just be quiet," he said, "and I'll bring you some supper in three minutes."

He slipped out of the stall and ran down toward the grain room.

"Better get the hay first," he thought. "It's getting dark fast."

He climbed up the narrow steps to the loft, trying to dodge the water that dripped upon him from a leak overhead. The loft was dark and the smell of sweet damp hay was even stronger here.

He felt his way over to the bales of peanut vines stored along the sides and pulled out an armload of them. He walked carefully down the steps and carried the hay to Fast Buck's stall. He threw the vines over into the hayrack, making sure that Fast Buck could reach them through the

slats. Then he went back to the grain room and got three ears of corn which he put into the feed box beside the hayrack.

Fast Buck was chewing hay but he took a deep bite out of an ear of corn and before he could eat that had bitten it once again.

"The storm didn't bother your appetite, did it, old boy?" He patted the pony. "Mustn't eat too much."

He went back into the grain room, found a bucket and filled it with water at the spigot outside the barn. By the time he got back to the stall the barn was almost completely dark. He could hardly see where to place the bucket. He pushed it far back into the corner below the hayrack. Fast Buck paid no attention but continued to eat the corn.

"Okay, Fast Buck. It's there if you want it. I'll be back to see you first thing in the morning. You belong to Mr. Taylor, but I'll take good care of you."

He thought suddenly of Mama's words this morning when she had told him how sometimes a thing wasn't cherished properly if it didn't belong to you. Cliff paused and thought over everything he might do to make Fast Buck comfortable. He had dried him off and fed him. There was water in the bucket. The stall was dry and clean. He could think of nothing else.

He gave the pony a quick pat and then went out to the edge of the barn hallway. He stood there for a long moment, hesitating as he looked at the lights in the back of the house. It was still raining softly. Now and then the whole sky would brighten as if a giant electric bulb had been turned on and off quickly, and the thunder rolled in the distance with disturbing giant tones.

Cliff drew a deep breath. Mama was going to ask where

he had been so long, how he got back, why he hadn't noticed the storm cloud. How could he tell her? He turned to look back into the stable. It seemed a wide black cavern of safety. Maybe it would be better to stay out here all night and take Fast Buck back early in the morning. For a moment he weighed the wisdom of this and then put the idea aside. He couldn't stay out here all night. Mama would have the whole countryside out looking for him at daybreak. Maybe she was already beginning to think of that.

Cliff caught his breath between his teeth, braced himself for what might come, and went running through the rain toward the house. His mother was peering anxiously out the screen door as he hit the back steps.

"Cliff Morgan, where on earth have you been until this hour of the night?" Her hands were on her slender hips and her face reflected her exasperation.

He brushed past her out of the rain onto the porch, shaking the water out of his eyes.

"I walked down to Mr. Taylor's," he said.

"I thought you were working in the garden and you were supposed to help me with the beans. Remember? Do you know it's after eight o'clock? Your daddy was just getting ready to go out and look for you."

"Daddy? Is he home?" Cliff felt an increasing weight of uneasiness.

"He came in about a half hour ago and we were getting so worried about you."

Cliff's mind searched quickly. It was one thing to keep Mama from knowing about the pony. It wasn't likely that she would go out to the barn, but Daddy was a different problem.

"Oh, lordy," Cliff thought. "What am I going to do?"

"You're soaking wet," Mama said. "Hurry and get out of those clothes. Then take a bath and come into the kitchen and get some supper."

She walked back toward the kitchen and Cliff could hear her still fussing: "I don't see why you couldn't see that big cloud making up. You should have started home sooner."

Cliff fled to his room and stepped gingerly out of his wet clothes. He spent a long time in the tub, dreading to come out and meet his father face to face. He was still squeezing suds out of the bath cloth onto his chest when he heard a knock on the bathroom door.

"Hey, Cliff." It was Daddy's voice. "Did you run down the drain with the water?"

"No, sir," said Cliff, trying to measure the degree of Daddy's irritation. He didn't sound so mad.

"Come on out and get your supper so Mama can get through in the kitchen."

That sounded a little tougher. "Yes, sir," Cliff said. Still he dawdled, stalling for time. Daddy called him again.

"Cliff, come on out. I want to talk to you. I want to know what's been going on out there in the lot."

Cliff's heart gave a big jump and his head jerked to attention. Did Daddy already know?

He jumped out of the tub and dried himself off quickly. Might as well get this over. But when he reached the kitchen he sidled in warily, easing into his chair. Daddy sat at the end of the table, one leg crossed casually over the other, his arms behind his head. He seemed relaxed and Cliff let out the long breath he had been holding.

"You came home late and worried your mother. I want to talk to you about that later," said Daddy pleasantly enough, "but I want to find out what you've been doing."

"What do you mean?" said Cliff quickly, on guard again.

Mama set a tall glass of milk, a slice of ham, some hot rolls, and potato salad before him.

Cliff looked at his father.

"I want to know what you and Hoke have been doing around here since I left."

"Oh," said Cliff. "That."

"Well," said Daddy. "Did you help Hoke with the feeding? Did you help him work the garden? Is the field of hay ready to harvest? Did you get the barn roof patched?"

Cliff laughed a little, partly with relief. "Well, I guess we didn't have time to do all of that, but we did some of it. I worked out most of the garden. It's pretty grassy with all the rain there's been lately. Hoke said it has really been a wet season. He wanted to get the barn roof patched, but I'm sure he didn't do anything on that this afternoon."

"What has he been doing?"

"I don't know. We fed up."

"Did he finish the spraying?"

"I don't know, sir."

"Why don't you know about some of these things?"

"Well, he left this morning and said he had some other work to do but he would get to the spraying if he had time. The sprayer was at his house when I went to Mr. Taylor's." Cliff was bolting down his food between answers.

"Where was Hoke?"

"I don't know. I thought maybe he was eating his lunch or asleep or something. His car was there, but I didn't see him anywhere."

"Well, I guess it will be a good thing if he didn't get to the spraying today. This hard rain would have washed the poison right off. Did he bring the sprayer back here?"

"I don't know, sir."

"You didn't look when you were out at the barn?"

"No, sir."

"Well, what were you doing out there?"

"I don't know, sir. I came in by the back way and it was raining so hard I was just in a hurry to get in the house." Cliff could not look at Daddy. He kept pushing his fork around on his plate although all his food was gone.

Daddy stood up. "I'd like to know if he did that spraying. I expect to be here all day tomorrow and I can help him with it. It's got to be done. Maybe we can step out to the tractor shelter and barn when the rain slacks up. We can see what the situation is out there." He looked out the open kitchen door across the porch into the darkness.

Cliff got up quickly and went outside. He could hear the soft rustle of rain against the trees. "Oh, it's really pouring down," he said. "We'd really get drowned going out there now."

"Don't go back out there and get soaked again tonight," said Mama.

Daddy turned back toward the kitchen and once more Cliff breathed a sigh of relief, but he remained at the doorway looking out toward the barn, seeing nothing but the glisten of rain on the leaves where light from the kitchen touched them. The knowledge that Fast Buck was out in the stable weighed heavily on his heart. It was really no fun having a pony in the stable when you had to feel so guilty about it, he thought miserably.

"I'll get up early in the morning and take him back home before anybody else gets up," he thought. "I never should have ridden him home."

10

FAST BUCK

The house was quiet when Cliff slipped out the back door the next morning. The clouds were gone but the sun was not yet visible above the horizon and blue mist hung above the fresh green fields. Drops of crystal moisture clung to his feet as he ran across the grass in the yard toward the barnyard.

He stepped his way around the puddles of water in the lot and slowed his pace at the entrance of the hallway. He walked quietly down the passage toward the stall. He wanted to see what Fast Buck would be doing with no one around. Not a sound came from the stall. He reached the door and stood on tiptoe to look over the top. Fast Buck lay quite still on the floor of the stable.

"Still asleep, huh?" he said. "Wake up, lazybones. I'll get you some breakfast. I bet you're hungry." He waited for the pony to get to his feet. Fast Buck did not stir.

"Hey, you, in there," Cliff said. He unfastened the latch to the door and stepped over the threshold. "Get up." He patted Fast Buck's rump and the pony lifted his head but then it fell back to the floor. Cliff looked at the pony in alarm.

"Fast Buck, what's the matter?" He stepped around to the pony's head and rubbed his muzzle. "Get up, old boy. I've got to take you home."

Fast Buck lifted his head and Cliff patted his neck, urging him to get to his feet but the pony's head fell back again. Panic seized Cliff. Something terrible was wrong. Fast Buck was acting funny.

"Oh, lordy," said Cliff. "What's wrong, Fast Buck? Can't you stand up?" He put his arms around the pony's neck and tried to lift his head. Fast Buck jerked his head away, pulled his front feet under himself and pushed himself up part way. Then he fell back as if the effort were too much for him. Cliff stood up and looked down at the pony with cold fear making bumps rise on his arms. Fast Buck was sick.

"Oh, please, Fast Buck. What's the matter? Please don't be sick." Cliff stared at the pony in despair. "Oh, gosh. Oh, my. What am I going to do?" He looked wildly about the stable. The bucket was still half full of water. The corn and hay were all gone. Nothing else was changed. What was wrong? What could have happened?

"I've got to do something," Cliff said aloud. "I can't just stand here." He felt sick in the pit of his stomach.

"I've got to go tell Daddy. If I don't Fast Buck may die." The awful thought occurred to him, "Suppose he dies anyway." Cliff almost sobbed aloud.

"Oh, please, Fast Buck. Hold on. I'll go get some help from somewhere."

He went racing across the barnyard toward the house.

"Daddy. Daddy," he howled. "Oh, Daddy. Wake up. I need some help."

His father was just coming leisurely out onto the porch when Cliff reached the steps. He was tucking his shirt into his blue jeans.

"Hey, you're up early," he said.

"Oh, Daddy," Cliff said, half crying. "I'm in trouble and I need some help."

The sleepy look dropped from Daddy's eyes. "What's wrong?" he asked quickly.

"It's Fast Buck. He's Mr. Taylor's pony. I rode him home last night. I think he's sick and I'm scared he's going to die." Cliff beat one fist against the palm of his other hand in his agony of anxiety.

Daddy was out the door and down the steps in an instant, crossing the muddy lot with long strides.

"Where is he?"

Cliff raced ahead of him toward the stall.

"In here," he said. He flung the door open and Daddy stepped inside.

"Get up," Daddy said sharply and he struck the pony soundly on his hip. Fast Buck jerked up, struggled to his feet, and stood up.

Cliff felt his heart leap as relief poured over him. "He's all right, isn't he?" Daddy's troubled face gave him the answer.

"No, sir. He certainly is not," Daddy said. "He's as sick as he can be. Did you feed him anything?"

"Yes, sir. I gave him three ears of corn and some pea-nut-vine hay."

"Peanut vines? Were they all right? Were they wet?"

"I don't know. I got the hay from the loft," Cliff said and then he remembered. "It could have been wet," he said miserably. "The roof was leaking."

"If he's had wet peanut vines, it means real trouble," Daddy said. He strode past Cliff and out of the stable.

"What are you going to do?" Cliff asked, hurrying to keep up with him.

"First, I'm going to call a veterinarian. Then we're going to work on that pony and after that, you and I are going to have a talk," said Daddy. His face was stern and troubled.

"Oh, Daddy, I'm so sorry," said Cliff. "I didn't think. I didn't know—I didn't mean—I don't know what to say."

"Time enough to do our talking later, Cliff. You get Mama to have hot water ready when the doctor comes, in case he needs it and you come back out to the barn. I want you to know everything that goes on out there."

"Yes, sir," Cliff said. He followed Daddy who bounded up the steps in one leap and went in to telephone the veterinarian.

It seemed forever until Dr. Harrington drove into the yard. Cliff left the pony who was breathing with great difficulty and went to open the gate to the barnyard. The doctor drove his car close to the barn hallway where Daddy had Fast Buck standing with a halter on.

The doctor was small and neat with a round pleasant face. His hands were gentle and quick as he examined the pony, his manner brisk and certain as he asked Cliff questions.

"Looks pretty bad," he said finally. "Those wet peanut

vines swell up when they get inside the stomach and make a hard ball that stops up his digestive tract completely. This makes a lot of gas that presses on the heart."

"Is it dangerous?" Cliff asked anxiously. "Will he die?"

"If he can't get rid of those peanut vines, he will," the doctor said. "His heart can't stand the pressure of that gas."

He opened the back of his car and stepped into a one-piece overall suit that covered all his clothes.

"Let's get a nip on him," he said to Daddy handing him a short stick with a loop of rope threaded through an eye at the end of it. Then he took a bucket and poured liquid into it from several bottles, stirring the mixture well.

"What's that you're going to give him?" Cliff asked.

"It's one gallon of mineral oil, one-half pound of epsom salts and I have added one-half ounce of chloral hydrate for his pain. This is a laxative and I hope it works," the doctor said.

Daddy had caught the pony's upper lip in the looped rope and had twisted it until it was tight. Fast Buck could no longer move his head without pulling his lip painfully.

He stood quite still while Dr. Harrington put a long rubber tube into his mouth and worked it down the pony's throat. He inserted a funnel in the end of the tube that protruded from his mouth and then he poured the liquid into the funnel. He rubbed the pony's throat as the liquid went down, then stepped aside and looked at the pony for a moment.

"That's fast-acting laxative," he said, "but we can't wait on it. I'll have to give him an enema and I'll need some warm water and some sweet soap."

Cliff ran to the house and came back with a bucket of hot water that Mama had ready. He watched the doctor swish the soap around in the water until he made a good suds and then he stood by while the doctor gave Fast Buck an enema.

"You can take the nip off, now," he said to Daddy. "We'll just wait a while and see if that helps him get rid of the vines."

The minute Fast Buck was released his front legs buckled under him and he sank to his side. Once on the ground he began to writhe. He kicked his legs and rolled over from one side to the other. Cliff watched the doctor's face which regarded the pony with a serious expression.

"Is he all right?" Cliff felt he had to ask again.

"No. He's not all right. You can see he's in a lot of pain," the doctor said. "The pressure is almost more than he can stand. Let's get him on his feet and walk him around. It's better for him not to lie down. That makes the pressure on his heart more dangerous."

Daddy and Dr. Harrington prodded the pony until he gathered strength to get on his feet again. Dr. Harrington handed the halter rope to Cliff.

"You keep him walking for awhile. Maybe that will help loosen up those vines so they will pass on out."

For an hour or more Cliff walked about the barnyard leading Fast Buck who kept trying to stop and lie down. There was no result either from the laxative or the enema. Cliff urged the pony to keep moving, talking to him gently in anxious tones.

Finally, Fast Buck refused to take another step. His front legs folded under him and he rolled over on his side. The doctor shook his head and then reached into the back of his car. He took out a long needle.

"What's that?" Cliff asked in alarm.

"This needle is called a trocar," said Dr. Harrington.

"It has a long hollow all the way through it. This pony has got to have some relief and I am going to let some of the air out of his stomach. It's about the last thing I can do for him."

He thrust the needle directly into the pony's side with a hard quick jab. Instantly a loud whish of air exploded from the pony filling the barnyard with a sour acrid odor.

The pony lay quite still for a time and then the doctor said, "Let's get him up again, Cliff, and keep him moving."

Again they prodded Fast Buck to his feet and Cliff walked him about the barnyard. Another hour passed and again the doctor inserted the needle to relieve the pressure and the pain that the pony suffered.

Cliff was at the far end of the barnyard when he saw Dr. Harrington close the back of his car and take off his coveralls in preparation to leave. He led the pony back toward the doctor.

"You're not leaving, are you, Dr. Harrington?"

"Yes, I have to make another call this morning," Dr. Harrington said. "But I'll come back if you need me. You can just call and my wife will get me wherever I am."

"Do you think he will be all right?" Cliff faced Dr. Harrington squarely, silently begging for some word of encouragement, some note of hope.

The doctor looked at Cliff. "He's got about one chance out of four to make it, Cliff. If he doesn't get relief, he'll be dead before tomorrow morning. If the treatment I gave him gets rid of the vines, by tomorrow morning he'll be as good as new and he'll be looking for another ear of corn." He walked around to the door of his car and got in.

"I've done everything I know to do. It's up to Fast Buck and the Lord, I guess. Though you can help some if you keep him walking."

Cliff watched Dr. Harrington go, aching with panic and distress, and there was little relief from these feelings during the rest of the day as he and Daddy took turns walking the sick pony about the barnyard, watching him struggle to keep on his feet, seeing his gray coat grow more and more muddy and shabby as he occasionally fell to the ground and wallowed in an agony of pain.

Sometimes Daddy stopped to work on the sprayer with Hoke, but usually he was in the barnyard keeping a close watch on Cliff and Fast Buck.

At dusk, the pony was so much worse that Daddy called Dr. Harrington again. The doctor came quickly and once more inserted the needle to relieve the intolerable pressure. He expressed surprise that the pony had lived through the day.

At suppertime Daddy tried to urge Cliff to go in for his meal but Cliff would not even leave the pony. It was almost midnight before Cliff finally agreed to go inside. Fast Buck would no longer walk and Daddy said it was cruel to keep him on his feet. They left him lying in his stall, breathing heavily. Cliff lay down on his bed without undressing and there in the dark he cried himself to sleep.

It was barely daylight when he opened his eyes and he was halfway off the porch before he became fully awake. At the edge of the barn he stopped, bracing himself for what he might find. He was filled with a devastating wave of dread.

"I can't stand to find him dead," he thought. "I don't believe I can look." But even as he said it, he knew that he would move toward the stall. He had to know. He forced his footsteps down the hallway and peered through the dim morning light over the door of the stall.

Fast Buck was standing by the hayrack. His gray coat

was smeared and stained and rumpled, but he was standing up.

Relief poured over Cliff like a rush of cool water. A little chill of happiness ran up his spine.

"Oh, golly, Fast Buck. You made it. You really made it. Oh, glory be. You're all right." He pressed his head against the panel beside the door and filled his eyes with the wonder of this sight. As he watched, Fast Buck folded his front knees under him and remained kneeling with his back legs still erect for a moment.

Cliff felt a hand on his shoulder and he looked up to find Daddy standing beside him.

"Look, Daddy. He looks as if he's saying a prayer," Cliff said.

Daddy smiled just a little. "I guess you've said a few yourself during the last twenty-four hours."

"You're right about that," Cliff said. "Yes, sir. You're certainly right about that."

11

PONY PROJECT
AND A PROBLEM

Daddy had the talk with Cliff that same morning following breakfast as they sat on the back steps together. Mama
was washing dishes in the kitchen and Paul and Wesley
were playing in the swings in the back yard. Every now
and then, the little boys went to the fence to look at Fast
Buck who was nibbling at patches of grass along the fence
next to the yard just as though there had never been anything wrong with him. Cliff and Daddy had washed him
off and cleaned him up. Now he was drying in the warm
summer sunshine. As soon as he was combed down, Cliff
was to take him back home.

"It isn't that we minded having you ride the pony
home," Daddy said, "but there are several things that we

do mind. First of all, we don't like the fact that you felt you had to hide it from us. Why were you afraid to tell us you had come home on the pony?"

"I don't know," said Cliff. He looked his father directly in the eye. "I really don't know, Daddy. I was afraid you'd be mad."

"But why did you think we'd be mad?"

Cliff thought for a moment. "Well, the pony was borrowed and I knew you and Mama did not like to borrow anything. And Mr. Taylor is a white man—"

"That's got nothing to do with this, Cliff. After all, Mr. Taylor asked you to take the pony and keep him a few days. There was really nothing wrong with that. But this involves something that is basically more important—that is, hiding something you don't have courage to face. I don't like that." Daddy's dark eyes were serious and probing and Cliff's gaze faltered before them. He hung his head.

"Look at me when I'm talking to you, Cliff."

It took some courage to face those searching eyes. "If you had been honest enough to tell me about the pony, I would have checked him to see if his feed was all right because you have had no experience in feeding a pony. I would have helped you see that he was all right and all this might have been avoided."

Cliff nodded miserably, "Yes, sir."

"So you got into trouble because you were afraid— afraid to come right out with the facts. You were wrong not to let us know about the pony and you were wrong in the first place not to clear it with your mama before you went to Mr. Taylor's."

Cliff dug his toe into the sandy walk as his father talked.

"Another thing, you see, is this. You made big promises

about how you would help your mother when you got down here. But yesterday, you walked out on your work in the garden and were gone all afternoon. She was not only anxious about you, but she was depending on you to help her with the beans. And you knew it. Now the beans may get too big to put in the freezer before we can get back in that wet garden to gather them. Not only will we lose them, but we have a bill to pay the veterinarian for his two visits."

Daddy paused a moment and then he said, "I might add that you let me down a little, too. I need to depend upon you because Hoke doesn't always finish what I leave for him to do, and you're the only one I have to look after things outside and keep up with what's going on."

Tears filled Cliff's eyes and rolled down his cheeks, but his gaze did not falter again.

"So we're talking about responsibility, too. Your responsibility to the family. What you do or don't do is important to all of us. Can you see that?"

"Yes, sir," said Cliff. "I can see it now."

"Good," said Daddy. "If you can understand this, maybe something worthwhile will come out of all that's happened."

"I'm just so sorry," Cliff said. "I'd like to help with the doctor's bill. I still have the four dollars I made from the seed."

Daddy thought about that for a moment or two.

"All right," he said. "That's good. That will be a help. I know you worked hard for that money and it's hard to give it up to pay for a mistake, but maybe this will make you feel better. Maybe it will help you to understand what responsibility means. I'll let you pay that much on the bill and I'll take care of the rest."

Cliff bit his bottom lip, knowing how important every penny was to Daddy, too. He looked out toward the barn.

Daddy stretched out his long legs so that they rested on the sandy walk, too.

"I'll tell you what I'd like to do," he said. "I know how badly you want a pony and I would like to see how well you can accept responsibility when it comes to something that belongs to you. Suppose I give you the chickens as a project. They'll be yours, and what you make from them will be yours. They're already half grown. If you feed and water them regularly they will be ready to sell in four or five weeks. You can sell all the young roosters and keep the hens. They'll begin laying in the fall. You can sell the surplus eggs during the winter and save the money to buy a pony when you have enough."

Cliff looked back at Daddy, his eyes brightening. He brushed a tear from his cheek.

"It will take you some time to save enough because you'll have to pay for the chicken feed out of your income, but it shouldn't take too long. If Mr. Taylor has a pony that he'll sell for a reasonable price, maybe you'll have enough saved by Christmas. Certainly by next summer."

"Oh, I'd like that," said Cliff. "It won't matter how long it takes. I'll have something to look forward to. I'd even be willing to start with a little colt. It would be fun to raise one from the beginning."

"We'll take Fast Buck back this afternoon after you brush him out good. And you'll have to explain to Mr. Taylor what happened. I'm sure he'll understand and will be very thankful that Fast Buck pulled through."

"I don't mind telling him so much," said Cliff. "But I'm afraid he might not want me around his ponies anymore."

"That's something you'll just have to face," said Daddy. "No matter what you're afraid of, you tell him the facts. Tell him what a tough time Fast Buck had and what was done to help him get over it."

"I think it's one of God's miracles," said Mama as she passed them on her way to hang out a basket of wet clothes.

Mr. Taylor listened to Cliff's story of Fast Buck's illness. It wasn't easy to tell him, but Cliff kept thinking of Daddy's words about having courage to come out with the facts.

"I guess we're all lucky, Cliff," Mr. Taylor said to him. "It's bad to have to learn about feeding the hard way. I know you didn't want to give him the wrong thing."

"I didn't realize the hay was wet," Cliff said. "But I should have thought because I felt water dripping from overhead."

"Well, you've had your first lesson in the hazards of pony care," Mr. Taylor said. "There are not many dangers, as I told you, but those that come are usually quick and often fatal. I tease Ted about not knowing much, but he has really learned a lot. You stick around here and you'll pick up many things from him that'll help you when you buy your own."

He showed Cliff and Daddy around the lot and they looked at his registered mares, many of which had colts, some still in foal. He pointed out several that he planned to take to the big sale that was held during August, and he showed them some of his good mares that he planned to keep. One bright sorrel mare with a white mane and tail caught Cliff's eye.

"What's her name?" he asked.

"I call her Lady Red," said Mr. Taylor. "She's out of registered stock but the man who sold her to me never had her registered. She's had several good colts and she's looking for another any day, now. You can see she's got a beautiful head, small ears, and conformation as pretty as you'll see. If this mare was registered, I wouldn't take five thousand dollars for her."

Daddy looked at Mr. Taylor in amazement and Cliff drew in his breath sharply.

"She's a beauty, all right," Cliff said. "I'm anxious to get back home and start working on my chickens so I can get a colt from you later on."

"All right, Cliff. You just come up when you're ready and look over the lot. I'll try to be fair on the price."

Cliff spent the days that followed trying to make up for being irresponsible. He helped Mama cheerfully, taking care of the little boys when she needed him, helping with the vegetables that needed to be put in the freezer, sometimes even washing the dishes when she had other things to do. He knew that she was trying to adjust to life on the farm, but she never seemed to feel really a part of all that was going on and when Cliff noticed that she was quiet and thoughtful, he told her some of Hoke's stories or tried even harder to be helpful.

She was happier when Daddy was at home. He came home more often, now, and some days he was able to stay on the farm and help with things that had to be done. Cliff watched him work with Hoke, harvesting the wheat, dusting the peanuts with sulphur, patching the barn, and doing other odd jobs around the house, and Cliff loved to hear the two of them as they worked. They were full of jokes and laughter. Those were working hours

that Cliff looked forward to and he kept hoping that
Daddy would come in and tell them that he was giving
up his job for good.

In the evening after all the work was done they would
sit out on the big screened front porch. They would
watch the shadows of twilight creep across the fields bring-
ing the blue mist that hung over the land like scarves of
gauze. They would listen to the sleepy sound of the birds
as they settled down for the night. Occasionally, a mock-
ingbird who was nesting close by would sit in the biggest
oak tree at the corner of the house and give them an
evening serenade. Finally, as darkness fell upon them, they
would feel the air grow cool and moist. The sound of
rain frogs became a part of the evening winds that blew
across the porch. Sometimes Cliff could hear Hoke's
mellow voice floating in on the night air, the lonesome
sweetness of it making him ache and smile at the same
time.

"You don't think of him as being lonesome when he's
around during the day," Cliff said to Daddy one evening.

"He's not lonesome, Cliff. Don't you worry about that.
He's got lots of girls. They all want to marry him."

"He sings about them all the time. Why doesn't he
get married?"

"He was married once," Daddy said. "His wife died."

"Was she sick or did something happen to her? What
was the matter?"

"She died when her baby was born. Both of them died.
I guess that's why Hoke never wanted to try marriage
again."

Cliff thought about that some when he worked with
Hoke, but Hoke never seemed sad. It was hard for him

to be serious. He laughed about everything. He made the work seem like play.

He would say, "I went up to Bell's store today. Found a mess of little kittens in an old barrel at the back of the store. Funny thing was, an old hen was setting on them instead of the mama cat."

"Honest?" Cliff said. "A hen?"

"Yep. I couldn't believe it. I was standing there wondering how in the name of goodness that happened when Johnny Green came in and he saw me looking at the hen. He bent over and pushed aside her feathers to see how many eggs she had under her. He sort of pulled back and then he looked again and shook his head."

"What did you say to him?" Cliff asked.

"I said to him, 'Johnny, what do you think of that?' Johnny scratched his head like this." Hoke demonstrated. "And then he shook his head again and said, 'I don't know, but I guarantee one thing, I ain't gonna eat no more eggs.' "

Cliff knew then that it was all a joke that Hoke had heard somewhere but it was funny and Cliff laughed. Hoke laughed with him, so hard that Cliff couldn't stop laughing. Then they would get back to the job at hand, cleaning up farm implements, cutting weeds around the barn, fixing a bridge in one of the paths through the fields, patching the screen wire that Wesley had knocked out with his tricycle, and more than once Hoke let him drive the tractor when they were breaking up the fields where the wheat had been harvested.

Sometimes Hoke failed to show up when he said he would be there. He always explained it by saying he had a little business to look after. Cliff teased him and said

he had been off to see one of his girls. Hoke would laugh
and soon Cliff would hear him singing:

"All my girls are daffy
Crazy over me.
But you ought to see Miss Jenny
She's my honeybee."

Cliff knew that Daddy worried about Hoke's absence
on occasion. He began to come home more often and
Cliff heard him tell Mama that he was giving up his job
the first week in August. Cliff felt a secret joy, knowing
that Daddy would be there to shoulder the responsibility
that Cliff sometimes found heavy to carry. He knew that
Daddy's presence at home would make it possible for him
to spend more time with Ted and the ponies at Mr.
Taylor's, too.

Whatever Cliff had to do, his chickens came first. He
tended to them with much interest. There were ninety-
eight of them. Hoke said there had been one hundred
and three but five of them had died the first week or two.
By the time Cliff had been feeding them a week he could
almost name them. Some of them were different from
the others. One young rooster had a comb that was already
high and red. He liked to boss the others. Two of them
had funny feet. One was lighter in color than any of the
rest. One of the hens had most of her tail feathers pecked
out.

"The others didn't like her," he told Hoke, and they
felt sorry for her. Daddy bought the feed for his chickens
and a careful account was kept of all expenses so that Cliff
could pay him back when he sold some of them. He fig-

ured he could sell the young roosters for fryers by the end of August and this should give him almost a third of what he would need to buy a pony if it were reasonably priced. He worried about the chickens if they did not eat all he left in the feeders.

"I want them to be fat," he told Daddy. "If I sell them by the pound, I'll get a higher price."

His days were happy ones and the happiest hours were the ones he spent with Ted. Almost every day Ted came by on Cricket. Sometimes they climbed on Cricket's back together and roamed over the land of Occoneechee Neck. They stopped by to see Miss Ceeny who gave them cinnamon buns that were deliciously juicy with buttered brown sugar and cinnamon and had a few nuts sprinkled on top. They went over to Lem Wakefield's house and played with him a time or two. Lem went to school in Jackson and was in a grade lower than Cliff. He was quick in math and he knew a lot about the woods and Cliff liked him, but he had the feeling that Lem did not like to talk much when Ted was around.

Occasionally, they went fishing at Blue Hole Mill Pond where they caught bass and bream large enough to take home for supper. Mama and Ted's grandmother packed lunches for them so they could stay long enough to catch some for the whole family.

Some days they let Paul and Wesley ride Cricket in the barnyard, always holding on to Wesley but sometimes letting Paul try it alone around the lot. Cliff could see how quickly his little brother had responded to the sunshine and country life. His cheeks had filled out, his eyes were brighter and he was always full of laughter now.

Sometimes Cliff and Ted just sat in the shade of the

oak trees at the edge of the barnyard and talked. They talked about fishing and swimming and experiences they'd had at school. They discussed music they liked and books they'd read and food they liked to eat. The only thing they did not discuss was the difference in their races. Cliff thought about it sometimes. He wondered how Ted really felt about playing with a Negro, but if Ted thought about it, he never mentioned it. They were so busy having adventures, sharing laughter, and being curious about the mysteries of the Occoneechee Neck that there seemed to be no place or time when race seemed an important matter to discuss.

The hours were full of endless happiness and Cliff awoke each morning eager for whatever the day would bring.

It was on Friday morning toward the last of July when he rose early to the sound of a young rooster crowing. The note was shrill and cracked. Cliff giggled. "He's trying," he said, "but he can't carry much of a tune."

"Listen to that rascal crow," he told Daddy who was already at home for the weekend and was getting up early with Cliff.

"He's learning," said Daddy, "but he doesn't hit the low notes very well."

"It sounds like he's saying, 'Happy birthday,'" said Cliff.

"Sounds to me like he's saying, 'I want my breakfast.'"

Cliff laughed. "I guess I'll go ahead and fill up their feeders before Mama gets our breakfast ready," he said and he ran down the back steps and out to the chicken house.

At the door he stopped short and stared at his chickens with horror. Dead chickens littered the floor of the chicken house. He counted them. Eleven lay lifeless on the ground. Most of the other chickens were huddled together in the back of the chicken house.

For a long moment Cliff stood looking at them, numb with shock, trying to convince himself that the chickens could not be dead. He stepped over the sill which had a small opening cut in it and picked up one of the chickens by a foot. Its body was cold but it was still limp, and the head dangled crazily as he ran back toward the house.

"Daddy," he called. "Come here. Quick. Something terrible has happened."

Daddy came out onto the porch and Mama stepped out beside him. Cliff ran up on the porch, still holding the chicken. Daddy took it from him and looked at it with a frown between his eyes.

"Oh, Daddy. I don't know what's the matter. There are ten more just like this out there."

"Ten?" said Daddy.

"Ten of them," Cliff said in tones of desperation. "Was their feed wrong, too? I fed them yesterday just like I have everyday." His eyes and voice were filled with despair.

Daddy turned the chicken over and examined it carefully. Cliff could see nothing wrong, but Daddy looked at its neck more closely and then he shook his head.

"No, Cliff. The feed had nothing to do with it this time. Looks to me as if a prowler visited your chicken house last night."

"But who would have been mean enough to just kill the chickens and leave them all over the ground like that?" Cliff asked. He was completely bewildered.

"It wasn't a person, Cliff. I think it was a weasel."

12

TRAP FOR A NIGHT PROWLER

Cliff searched his mind trying to remember what he knew about weasels as Daddy walked down the back steps and laid the chicken on the ground in the back yard. Cliff ran down the steps after him and Mama came out, too. They bent over the chicken as Daddy turned it over and pulled aside the feathers.

"Look at this," Daddy said. He showed them a tiny slit at the base of the neck. "The weasel is a killer. He cuts into the neck and sucks out the chicken's blood."

Cliff looked at his daddy with an expression of horror. "And that's all he wants? They're lying all over the ground out there. He didn't even try to eat them."

"No, He often kills just for the love of it. Chickens, ducks, rats, birds—they're all afraid of the weasel."

"I can understand that. You should see what he's done," said Cliff.

"Let's go look," said Daddy.

He and Cliff walked back out to the chicken house and Mama went with them to see what had happened.

"What does a weasel look like?" Cliff asked, almost running to keep up with Daddy.

"He is a slender brown creature with a long head and neck that looks sort of snakelike. He weaves his head back and forth until he can strike his victim in a vital spot. Up north they turn white in the winter and ermine coats are made from their fur."

"How did he get in the chicken house, do you suppose?"

"He can slip through most any hole that a snake can get through," said Daddy, pointing to the hole that was cut out under the door so the chickens could pass through to the chicken yard. "He's pretty cunning and deadly where chickens are concerned."

"I can't believe one weasel would kill so many in one night," Mama said as they stood looking down at the dead chickens.

"It takes only one to do the damage," Daddy said. He piled the chickens in a heap at the door while Cliff looked on dismally.

"Suppose he comes again. He could kill all my chickens."

"That's exactly what he'll do," said Daddy grimly. "And you can bet your bottom dollar he'll be back tonight and the next night, too."

"What are we going to do?" Cliff's words were a wail.

"I don't know," said Daddy, "but we'll have to do

something or you'll wind up with no chickens." He put his hand on Cliff's shoulder. "We're certainly not going to sit down and let him have them without putting up some kind of a fight. Let me think about it," he said as they walked back to the house together.

"Uncle Ed had lots of steel traps," Cliff said. "They're out in the gear room. Maybe we can catch him with one of those."

"We'll see," said Daddy. "Give me time to think."

During the afternoon, Daddy and Cliff tried to work out the problem together.

"If I set traps without putting the chickens somewhere else the chickens will step in the traps," Daddy said.

"Could we put the chickens in the crates that Uncle Ed stored up in the barn loft?"

"Yes," said Daddy. "That's a lot of trouble but we could do that." Then he shook his head. "We'll have to leave a few for bait and they might still step on the traps."

"Maybe we could put a little fence around them inside the chicken house."

Daddy listened thoughtfully. "That's a good idea," he said. "You're using your head, Cliff. Let's try that."

Ted came up while they were working and helped them set up a four-foot wire fence with small mesh to hold the chickens. At dusk when the chickens came to roost, they caught all but three and put them in crates Uncle Ed had used for carrying his chickens to market. The remaining three were put inside the fence that was about four feet in diameter.

Daddy set two steel traps, one outside the small hole cut below the door and one inside.

"Don't you boys forget and step in one of these traps

now," said Daddy. "They're not playthings. They're dangerous."

He covered both the traps with straw so that they were not visible. "This fellow is a pretty smart animal but maybe all this will do the trick."

"He's bound to step on one of them," Ted said, admiration in his voice. "I just know you'll catch him before he gets to the chickens this time."

He left on Cricket, promising he would be back early the next morning to see if they had the weasel. "I've never seen one," he said. "It will be something to tell the fellows at school—about how we caught a wicked chicken-thief."

Ted's shrill whistle awoke Cliff the next morning and he bounced out of bed and flew to the window. Ted was waiting outside the fence on Cricket.

"Wait a minute. I'm coming," Cliff called out.

"Hurry up," said Ted. "I can't wait to see what you caught."

Cliff heard Daddy up in his room as he pulled on his clothes quickly and ran barefooted out the back door. Ted had tied Cricket to the fence and was waiting at the foot of the back steps. They raced across the barnyard and stopped short outside the chicken house. The first trap outside was undisturbed.

Cliff took a stick and brushed aside the straw that lay over the steel trap. The trap snapped, catching the stick in its jagged teeth. The boys jumped.

"He got by that one," Ted said.

"I bet the one inside caught him," Cliff said. "It had to."

He opened the door cautiously. The straw over the

second trap lay undisturbed, too. Cliff looked quickly inside the fence they had erected and his mouth flew open in dismay. Inside the fence the three chickens lay limp and lifeless. Otherwise, not a thing was disturbed.

"How about that!" Ted said. "He killed all three of them."

"I can't believe it. I can't believe he missed both traps," said Cliff.

Daddy appeared at the doorway.

"Look," Cliff said. "Look what he's done. He climbed the fence and got all three of the chickens. He never even touched the traps."

Daddy stood looking and then shook his head. "He may have been small enough to slip through this fine mesh wire," he said, "and he was clever to get by those traps."

"Do you still think it really is a weasel, Daddy?" Cliff asked.

"I'm sure of it," Daddy said. "He's a pretty cunning animal and he just outsmarted us, that's all. You've heard of somebody weaseling out of something, haven't you? That means they're slick and sharp at getting around something. We've got to be a little bit smarter if we want to catch this fellow."

Work of the day had to go on. Ted helped Cliff feed the chickens that were cooped up uncomfortably in the crates. Cliff knew that he could not keep them there long and he felt frustrated that they had to wait until night to do anything about the weasel.

"If we don't catch him tonight I just can't stand it," he told Ted. "I have only eighty-four left out of the ninety-eight. I can't stand to lose anymore."

They mapped out a new plan of attack. Daddy dug a circular pit two feet in diameter and at dusk he put two of the chickens down in it. He covered the pit with fine screen wire and they fastened this down securely with stakes. Around this pit Daddy set five steel traps which could not be seen under the tiny mounds of straw. Then the four-foot fence was set up again outside the traps.

"If that doesn't get him," Cliff said, "I really don't know how we'll ever catch him."

"We can't keep those other chickens cooped up much longer either," said Daddy. "They aren't faring too well like that."

Ted went home that evening promising to be back again the first thing in the morning.

Cliff could hardly sleep that night. Several times he awoke and his first thought was of his chickens. He wanted to get up and go out with a flashlight to see what had happened but he was afraid he might scare off the weasel which would mean setting the traps another night. He got up once and went to his back window, straining to hear any sound that might betray the presence of the animal, but he heard only the distant sound of rain frogs. And he could hardly contain his anxiety when he awoke before dawn. Daddy was already up and together they hurried out to the chicken house.

They stepped inside and looked at the pit and the traps they had set, then looked at each other mystified. It appeared that nothing had been touched.

The chickens were safe inside the pit where Daddy had put them and the straw over the traps was hardly disturbed.

"He must not have come last night," Daddy said, his voice reflecting disappointment.

But Cliff looked more closely at the little mounds of straw that covered the traps. One of them was flatter than the others. Cliff picked up a long stick and pushed aside the straw very gently. The trap that had been set there was gone. There was nothing, absolutely nothing, beneath the straw.

Cliff and Daddy looked at each other again.

"It's gone," Cliff said.

"He took it with him," Daddy said.

"How could a weasel do that?" Cliff asked. "How could he go off with a trap?"

"He climbed the fence," said Daddy, "but that trap went with him, somehow."

Cliff thought about that for a long time. Somewhere out in the woods back of their house was a weasel with a steel trap attached to one leg or one foot, or perhaps, to his tail.

"Serves him right," said Ted when he came up later, "for killing all your chickens. Now maybe he'll bear the mark of a chicken-killer forever."

They laughed a little about that, but Cliff kept thinking about the little woods creature dragging the trap around and in spite of his relief, as the days passed, that his chickens were no longer bothered, he felt sad for the weasel who might be wearing a steel trap around everywhere he went.

13

SEARCH FOR THE KILLER

Cliff and Ted went looking for the weasel. They talked about it for almost a week before they finally decided to go.

"I'm just curious to know if he still has that trap on his leg," Cliff said.

It was the first week in August and they planned their trip to the woods as they sat on Cliff's back porch eating cookies and drinking lemonade that Mama had made. The grain had been harvested, cotton and peanuts were laid by except for occasional spraying that had to be continued right up until the bolls began to open. Mama had her freezer full of vegetables and there was very little that could be done on the farm or around the barnyard. Daddy was giving up his job at the end of this week and Hoke came only rarely to help with the chores now.

Mama packed a lunch for the boys one morning while Cliff was finishing up his work outside. Cliff made sure that there was enough feed and water for the chickens and for the little pigs which were big enough, now, to eat a little along with their mother.

Ted came racing up the lane on Cricket at ten o'clock and Cliff was outside ready to climb on the pony before he could even stop. Mama came out and gave Cliff a knapsack which he threw over his shoulder.

"There are some sandwiches and some candy bars and a couple of pieces of fried chicken for each of you in there," she said. "I've put in the little Thermos jug with milk. I think that'll be enough for a lunch."

"That's fine, Mrs. Morgan," said Ted. "That'll taste mighty good about twelve o'clock."

"I have some corn-field peas all shelled out in here. Do you suppose your grandmother would like to have some? You can take them to her when you bring Cliff back if she'd like to have them."

"I'm sure she would. She likes them better than any other vegetable and so do I," he said grinning. "She doesn't have any this year. I'll take them now if you want me to."

"You reckon we'll have time?" Cliff asked. He was impatient to be off to the woods.

"Sure. It won't take us two minutes to go by there," Ted said. "We can go up through the pasture and come back to one of the paths that goes down through the woods between Hoke's house and Granddaddy's pasture."

Mama went back into the house and came back out to the fence that separated the back yard from the farm path. She carried a two-quart tin pail with a handle. She handed it up to Cliff who was already sitting behind Ted on Cricket.

"Tell her she can get more whenever she wants some," Mama said. "She's been so good to share her nice apples with me."

"Yes, ma'am. I'll tell her. I know she'll be glad to get them."

Cliff held the bucket that bumped awkwardly against his legs as Ted turned the pony around to go back to the lane that skirted the river woods.

"You boys be careful," Mama called after them. "Don't run that pony through the woods and get knocked off."

"Okay," Cliff called back gaily. His words were snatched from his mouth and lost in the wind as they galloped around the corner and down the dusty lane toward Mr. Taylor's.

At the corner of Mr. Taylor's pasture nearest the woods, Ted drew the pony to a halt.

"You've got the bucket. Hold Cricket while I unfasten the gate. We'll go through this pasture and save a little time."

He slid off the pony's back and Cliff picked up the reins in his left hand. When Ted had opened the gate he rode the pony through and waited for Ted to fasten it. He could see some of the mares grazing far up at the front of the pasture next to the barnyard and he gazed at them wistfully, thinking how nice it would be when he had one grazing around his house. Ted leaped up behind him.

"We'll be coming right back. No need to fasten the wire back around the latch. I think it'll hold, no longer than we'll be gone."

They raced across the pasture, scattering the mares as they rode past them. Ted opened the gate and they went through to the barnyard back of the Taylor house.

Mrs. Taylor came out onto the back porch after Ted had carried the peas in to her. She watched while Ted once more got up on Cricket's back. She was a large woman with strands of gray hair that played about her broad pleasant face.

She smiled and waved at Cliff. "Tell your mother I'm so glad to get the peas," she said. "I'll have them for Ted's supper. Ted, if you're going back down to the woods, stop at the young corn field and tell your grand-daddy that Dr. Harrington called. He's coming down in about an hour to give those two ponies a shot before he takes them to the sale next week."

"Okay. We'll go that way," Ted called back and they were off, taking the dirt lane that passed the young corn field.

They stopped to deliver the message to Mr. Taylor and then they rode along the path until they came to a grassy opening that led down through the junglelike forest toward the river.

Ted slowed the pony to a walk and turned Cricket into the opening.

"Is this a road?" Cliff asked.

"It must have been once upon a time," Ted said. "It's pretty grown up with weeds and grass."

Sunlight and shadow dappled the earth where tall grass grew sparsely out of deep ruts. Trees on each side of the path towered above the boys as they rode Cricket between

them. Green vines crept through the woods and sometimes covered the undergrowth that grew among the trees.

"Wonder where the road goes?" Cliff mused.

"I don't know," said Ted. "I've never been down this
way. But we can follow it and find out."

"I imagine it goes straight to the river. Maybe somebody had a boat landing down there once," said Cliff.

The pony stepped gingerly over small limbs that had
fallen in the path, avoiding ruts skillfully, stopping now
and then to nibble at the long green blades of grass that
brushed his fetlocks.

The road wound endlessly, it seemed, bending east to
run parallel to the river and then curving back north in
the direction that led toward the river. Sometimes the
underbrush and vines were so thick they seemed to form
a dense wall on either side of the path.

"It's downright spooky," Ted said. "I bet you could
get lost in these woods."

As they drew closer to the river the trees seemed to
grow taller and straighter. There were fewer small trees,
but lush vines spread over the earth and circled huge tree
trunks, cascading down from the limbs in flowing billows
of green foliage.

"Look," said Ted. "There's an opening in those vines.
It looks almost like the opening to a cave. Want to go
through there?"

"No, let's follow the path," Cliff said. "Maybe we'll
come back this way and we can go through there then."

At last, the road came to the river's edge. The upper
bank where huge trees grew horizontally over a lower bank
was high above the river. Below them was a second lower
bank covered with a skimpy growth of tall grass but almost
bare of trees. Below this was still another level along

which the reddish water of the Roanoke River lapped at the narrow clay shore.

Crude steps made of clay, long unused, led from the upper bank to the middle bank. This middle bank stretched endlessly to each side of them like a long hallway beneath trees that grew from the upper bank straight toward the river like rafters, and overhead there was a canopy of green foliage that swept like the sides of a tent down to the water's edge.

"It doesn't seem likely there would be a weasel's house around here," Cliff said. "How in the heck are we going to look for him?"

"He very likely lives close to water," said Ted. "I think we'd come nearer finding him close to some still water like a pond or something."

"Do you know whether or not there is a pond in these woods?" Cliff asked.

"No. I've never heard Granddaddy say anything about it. Anybody who wants to fish usually goes to Blue Hole Mill Pond."

Both boys knew that the mill pond where they had fished several times was on the other side of the highway, at least three miles from this point.

"The weasel must have come from somewhere in these woods up closer to the back of your house," said Ted.

"Let's walk up the river and look around a bit," said Cliff. "We might stumble into something somewhere along the way."

"What are we going to do with Cricket?" Ted asked. "I don't believe he can get down that steep bank."

Both boys looked at the embankment and they agreed it was too dangerous to try getting Cricket down to the middle level.

They found a grassy spot where Cricket could graze until they returned and they set out on foot to explore the river's edge. Sometimes they walked along the upper level of the bank, tearing their way through vines, jumping over tree limbs, and walking out over the middle bank on the horizontal tree trunks. Sometimes they slipped and slid down the clay bank to the middle level where they caught the long rattan vines and swung themselves far out over the lower bank of the river below.

Once Ted's hands slipped and he slid down a vine toward the water. Cliff gasped as he saw Ted kicking frantically to direct his plunge back toward the bank. He landed at the water's edge. Cliff reached down and helped Ted climb back up the middle bank and they lay exhausted and scared beneath the thick tree trunks that leaned down toward the water.

"Don't do that again," Cliff said to Ted. "That river's tough."

"Yeah. I know. Granddaddy said it was too treacherous to swim in."

"It's got hidden whirlpools in it," said Cliff, "and stumps along the edges that can snag a boat in a minute if you don't know where you're going."

"Granddaddy said it was great for rock-fishing in May and we caught a few when I first came in June but the spawning season is over now."

"I tried to get Hoke to take me fishing in the river," said Cliff, "but he said he wasn't one for fooling around in the woods and on the river."

They talked for awhile about fishing and sports at school and what they liked best about being on the farm and then they thought again of the weasel.

"Let's walk on up the river a little farther," said Cliff. "It's getting close to dinnertime, I think."

It was several hundred yards farther along the river that they found a deep crevice in the upper bank through which a small stream of water emptied into the river.

"Let's follow this and see where it comes from," Cliff said.

They scrambled up the bank to the upper level and followed the stream. Thick vines covered the banks which deepened into a narrow gorge as they got farther away from the river. They pushed their way through vines until they came to the edge of a deep cliff which dropped suddenly before them to a small pond that lay like a jewel below. The hill upon which they stood sloped gently downward around the pond until the land on the far side was level with the water. To their right was a cavelike opening in the ravine upon which they stood. There was a narrow sandy shore in front of it.

"It looks like a lake in the middle of pure jungle," Cliff said.

"Do you reckon anybody else has even been here?" Ted said thoughtfully.

"I doubt it," Cliff said, "but it's a perfect place for wild animals to come for water. Maybe the weasel has been here."

"It's a good place for a camp or a hideout," Ted said.

"It's a good place for us to eat lunch," said Cliff. "Let's walk around to the cave and that little shore in front of it."

They stepped through and over the vines until they reached a place where the ravine was low enough for them to jump to the edge of the pond. They explored the tiny cave and found it amply large to hold them.

"It would be fun to come down here and fish instead of going to Blue Hole," Ted said. "This could be our own private fishing pond."

"I wish we had brought fishing poles today," said Cliff.

"Anyway we can eat lunch here," Ted said. "Maybe if we sit here long enough the weasel will come to the pond."

The boys settled down outside the cave on the narrow bank beside the pond with their backs propped against the ravine. They took out their sandwiches and the chicken. Cliff poured milk into the double lids of the Thermos jug and handed one to Ted. They ate with relish, enveloped with a pleasant sense of adventure and comradeship.

14

DISCOVERY

The little raccoon crept up to the water's edge on the far side of the pond and stopped. His fat body was grayish brown and his bushy tail was encircled with black rings of heavy fur. He looked as if he had a black mask over his eyes.

"Look, Ted," Cliff whispered. "He has something in his mouth. He's come to eat his lunch. I thought they usually slept in the daytime. He must be hungry."

"I bet he's going to wash it first," said Ted.

The two boys sat motionless, watching in fascination. The raccoon looked to the right and to the left and then, crouching, he stretched out toward the pond and dipped into the water the object that he held in the slim fingers of his front paws. He swished it around vigorously, then drew it out and examined it carefully. He rubbed it with his paws and then dipped it into the water again and again.

Satisfied, at last, he sat back on his haunches and, looking thoughtfully about him, began to munch on his food. The boys watched in wonder until the little creature finished and went creeping back into the woods from which he had come.

"Gosh, he's cleaner than most folks." Ted giggled and they looked at each other. Neither of them had even thought of washing their hands before they ate. They burst out laughing and began to put away the scraps and paper they had left from their lunch.

For a time after they finished they lay relaxed, planning how they would come back to the pond with fishing poles and try their luck. But, at last, they thought about the weasel once more. Cliff threw the knapsack over his shoulder. Ted threw their chicken bones in the water and they began to circle the pond looking for tracks. There were only a few at the water's edge where the raccoon had sat while he ate his lunch and even these disappeared a few feet back from the pond where the mat of leaves and vines covered the earth.

It was while they were looking for tracks that they discovered a stream that flowed into the pond from the south. Running along beside it was what appeared to be a narrow path.

"It looks sort of like a path," Cliff said. "We can see where it goes."

"Looks snaky to me," Ted said.

But Cliff was already pushing his way through the underbrush and vines which grew along the faint path that was occasionally too obscure to be sure about.

"It's a path all right but it certainly hasn't been used in a long time," said Ted.

"I think it's a path that animals use," said Cliff. "We might run across the weasel anytime."

They had trouble following the path at times but they stayed close to the stream and the spirit of adventure kept them going. They walked with difficulty as vines grew in increasingly wild abandon and the path became less pronounced. They stopped now and then to look at some tree or a bird or squirrel, but nowhere did they find any trace of the weasel.

They had walked for what seemed miles when Ted said, "I think we'd better go back and get Cricket. He must be getting tired of waiting for us."

"I think we are going back in that direction now," said Cliff.

"I don't see how you can tell," said Ted. "You can't see the sun for all the trees."

"No, but we walked east along the river and then turned south to find the pond. We walked south away from that and this stream has been turning west so we're bound to be going back toward the old road we followed on Cricket."

"You're just making all that up. There's no way to tell which direction we're going and I don't want to get lost in these woods," Ted said.

"I don't see how we can get lost," Cliff said. "The farms are on one side of us and the river's on the other."

"I've always heard you walk in circles when you get lost in the woods," Ted said.

"As long as we follow this path we're going somewhere," said Cliff stoutly, though Ted was shaking his conviction.

"But I'm not even sure this is a path," Ted said. His steps had slowed. "We could be going anywhere and this woods is mighty big. We've been walking a long time and we haven't gotten anywhere yet." He stopped. "I think I'm going back the way we came."

"Wait," said Cliff. "Don't go yet. Let's go a little farther up this stream. If we don't come out somewhere soon, we'll turn around and go back."

Ted said nothing but he followed Cliff slowly. The vines were even thicker now and it was more and more difficult to push their way through. Shadows deepened, too, and Cliff's steps were more uncertain.

They came to a dense wall of vines that rose up in front of them. The stream seemed to disappear beneath the vines.

"I don't like this, Cliff," Ted said. "I'm ready to go back. I'm getting worried about Cricket."

Cliff was no longer sure that they were going in the right direction to get back to Cricket but he hid his concern.

"Let me look around on the other side of these vines. The stream is bound to go on somewhere and the path should, too."

Ted remained rooted to the earth where he was. "You can look if you want to but I'm not moving from this spot. I can't see any path anymore. If we lose this stream we'll never get back where we came from. I'm scared we're already lost."

"We can't be lost," Cliff insisted, but his words were braver than he felt.

"Well, it's a long way back the way we came and if

we're going back that way we better turn around now and get started before it gets dark."

Cliff began to push and hack his way through the wall of vines that fell like a heavy green blanket from the tall limbs overhead. He tore at the vines with his hands.

"Cliff." Ted's voice was a pleading wail. "I'm ready to go back. Suppose you step on a snake."

"This is a fine time to be worrying about that," said Cliff. "If we didn't see one back at the pond, we certainly won't see one here." He continued to pull at the vines which clung to each other with ironlike tendrils.

"I don't mind telling you I'm getting scared of snakes and scared of being lost and just plain scared of being here. I don't know where we are and you don't either."

"Look, Ted," Cliff said. "I think I'm getting through these vines."

"But where are you when you get through? There's probably just more vines." Ted turned and took a few steps back along the stream.

"Wait," said Cliff in sharp excitement. "There is something on the other side of these vines." His hands tugged at stubborn tendrils.

Ted stopped. "What is it?" he said, responding to the excitement in Cliff's tone.

"I don't know, but there's something in there."

"Is it alive?" Ted asked, moving back toward Cliff.

"I don't know what it is. But help me," said Cliff.

Ted moved up beside Cliff and began to help him tear the vines apart. They managed to penetrate the wall with an opening and they peered beyond an open area formed by a curtain of vines. It was as if a room with circular walls had been formed by the growth of vines that cascaded from tree limbs overhead.

Inside, the vines were flattened to the earth as if they had been walked on a great deal and they covered the ground like a green carpet. The stream ran along one side of the circular area, but the boys' attention was focused upon the center of the space where there was a strange contraption of metal and wood, and copper coils of piping that snaked down into a wooden barrel.

The boys stared at it in bewilderment.

"What is it?" Ted whispered.

"I don't know," Cliff whispered back. A strange feeling of uneasiness possessed him. "It looks like some kind of machinery."

"What's it doing out here in the middle of nowhere?"

"I don't know that either," Cliff said.

"At least we're not lost anymore," said Ted. "We know somebody had to put it here and if they got out, so can we. Let's get in there and see it better."

"Maybe we'd better not," said Cliff. He felt the unaccountable anxiety rising, but Ted was already pulling the vines to make the hole bigger so they could step through.

Inside the cleared green room they moved freely toward the strange mechanism. Directly in front of them as they approached were four barrels of grayish white substance that looked like wet cornmeal. A strange sour odor pervaded the air.

Farther over there was a big oil drum set up on a fire grate supported by iron legs. Under this were the charred remains of a fire. Pipes led from this drum to a barrel and from this second barrel ran another copper pipe which coiled down into a third barrel. From the bottom of this barrel a tiny pipe extended over a bucket. Cliff bent over the bucket and sniffed. An unmistakable odor filled his nostrils. Ted bent over and smelled, too. His head jerked up. His blue eyes were wide with shock and a sort of wicked excitement.

"Cliff," Ted said. "This is a whiskey still. That stuff in those barrels is mash."

"Yeah." Cliff nodded. A weak sickish feeling had begun to settle in the pit of his stomach. "That's exactly what it is."

"But whose could it be?"

Ted's words touched the spot that was beginning to ache within Cliff. This was exactly what troubled him. His mind was already making quick calculations. The still belonged to somebody and it was somewhere back of his home—back of the house that Uncle Ed had built. Cliff felt the painful idea turn over in his mind. Surely Uncle Ed had not made whiskey. But another thought was nagging at him. Uncle Ed had made a lot of money somewhere. Had he really made it all from farming and raising chickens? Or had he paid for the house with money made by selling whiskey? Cliff tried to put the idea aside but it was there and it would not go away. It was as if ocean waves of suspicion and distress were washing over him. He turned away from Ted. If Uncle Ed had made his money this way, he didn't want Ted to know. He wished he had not come in here. He did not want to be here— especially with Ted.

"What do you think, Cliff? Whose could it be?" Ted repeated. He was moving with curiosity from one barrel to the other, looking in.

"I don't know," Cliff said irritably. "But we better get out of here. At least we know somebody has been here and maybe we can find a way out." He realized he was

repeating Ted's anxious words spoken before they knew
this was a whiskey still and he felt angry with himself for
appearing eager to get out.

Ted no longer seemed in a hurry. His fear of being lost
was completely gone. He examined the still with great
interest saying he had never seen a still before, and how
complicated it all looked, and how he'd bet they could
find some whiskey, but Cliff began to look for a path
leading from the well-concealed area.

At first there seemed no way out and then his eyes fell
upon a path that led between layers of the vines. It was
as though a huge curtain closed at that point with one
side lapping over the other so that the well-trod pathway
between was almost undetectable.

"Here's the way out, Ted. I think we'd better go," he
said.

Ted followed him with reluctance, circling the vine-
covered room and finally backing out before he turned
to walk behind Cliff down a narrow path leading out.

"That's the smartest place to hide something like a
still I could ever imagine," Ted said. "I wonder whose
it is."

"I don't know," said Cliff shortly, not wanting to discuss it. "I don't know much about these people down
here."

He was moving along the path quickly now, anxious
to be away from the smothering walls of vines that rose
more loosely about them now, when he heard Ted gasp.
He turned quickly.

"Look at this, Cliff. This path goes two ways."

Sure enough, Cliff had walked right past a second path
that circled a big poplar tree and led off in another direc-

tion. Ted had already moved out of sight down the newly discovered path.

"Come on, Ted We've got to get back to Cricket." Cliff was impatient.

"Cliff," Ted called back with excitement. "There's an old house here. Come on." Now Cliff was reluctant, but he followed Ted down the path straight to the door of a small house so covered with vines that only the crumbling chimney and one end of the exposed weatherboards could be seen. Vines grew more sparsely up the trees around it.

"Looks like this hasn't been used for years," Ted said.

There was a crude wooden block for a step and some of the windows were cracked, but the door was fastened with a padlock.

"Whoever owns it doesn't want anybody going in it," Ted said. He tilted his head to one side with a cock of the eye and said, "That's funny."

"What's funny?" Cliff asked nervously.

"The house looks so old and deserted and all. But the padlock is new."

Cliff stared. The padlock was indeed shiny. Still, it might have been Uncle Ed's. It probably wouldn't have rusted in the weeks that had passed since Uncle Ed died.

"Aren't you a great detective, though?" he said to Ted. He tried to cover his distress with scorn and humor, but Ted looked at him curiously. Cliff laughed shortly and turned away from Ted who shrugged his shoulders and moved toward the window beside the door.

Ted pressed his face against the cracked windowpane. "Look, Cliff," he said.

Cliff peered inside, too. The floor of the small room

they looked into was covered with dust but it was empty. Cliff could see that there was a smaller room at the back for a door led into it. A narrow stairway at the side of the room led to an upper level.

"I don't see anything," said Cliff. But Ted had moved around a patch of tall ornamental grass growing wild at the corner of the house and he called back to Cliff.

"Hey, Cliff, this window will open. I'm going in."

Cliff walked around the corner. Ted was pushing up the window.

"I don't think we'd better do that," Cliff said.

"Why not? It's deserted," said Ted. He had already given himself a little jump and had his right leg over the windowsill as if he were mounting Cricket.

"Somebody might live here," said Cliff nervously.

"Now who's scared?" Ted said scornfully. "What kind of an excuse is that? You know it's not so."

Cliff put aside his doubts and followed Ted into the house.

It was in the loft above the small back room that they found the whiskey. It was stored in canning jars, rows and rows of them. Ted unscrewed one of the tops and they smelled it.

"I dare you to taste," he said.

Cliff shook his head. He was sick of the whole business and wanted to be out of the house and away from this place. He wanted to erase everything he had seen from his mind.

"I'll taste it," Ted said, giggling. His eyes were full of mischief and glee. He stuck his finger into the jar and put it on his tongue. Then he made a terrible face.

"Ugh," he said. "It's horrible." He screwed the top back on and stood up. "Whoever owns all this is really a big operator. I bet he makes a lot of money selling this stuff. Who could it be?"

"Let's get out of here, Ted," Cliff begged.

"You're right," Ted said. "Whoever made all this stuff may come back here any minute."

The thought was electric. Cliff stared at Ted. Maybe Uncle Ed had not made the whiskey. Maybe it did belong to someone else. If that were true it was possible that the owner might catch them here. His spine suddenly prickled and he felt a cold chill of fear.

"Yeah. Let's go."

They scampered down the steep little stairway and let themselves out through the open window.

15

THE QUARREL

Ted pulled down the window of the little shack and he and Cliff turned to walk back down the path toward the poplar tree where they had found this route. They had taken only a few steps when Cliff stopped short. He held up his hand and stopped Ted who was walking behind him.

"Hush, Ted. I heard something."

The boys stood quite still. There was a rustling sound in the vines farther up the path.

"Somebody's coming," Ted whispered back.

In desperation they looked about them and with one accord they pressed through an opening in the scanty growth of vines beside them and were swallowed by the foliage as if they had melted into it. They stood motionless, hardly breathing as the rustle of footsteps, muted by the thick forest cover of leaves and vines, passed quite close to them and moved toward the house.

They heard someone stop at the front door. There was a quiet grunt as if someone exerted great force and there was silence.

"Can you see who it is?" Ted breathed in Cliff's ear. He reached across Cliff's shoulder and parted the leaves of the vine. They peered through the tiny opening.

A big sack had been set on the ground while a man beside it unlocked the door. They could see only his back. They heard the click of the padlock as it flipped open and saw the man turn to pick up his sack. They could see his face clearly now and both boys gasped.

"It's Hoke!" said Ted. "He's got a bag of sugar."

Cliff nodded, a great wave of sickness washing over him as bits of knowledge began to fall into place. Sugar was needed to make whiskey. The still belonged to Hoke. Hoke was making whiskey in his spare time. That was where he spent the hours when he wasn't helping Daddy. That was why they couldn't find him sometimes when they needed him. Cliff felt a great pain settling in his chest. How could anybody as nice as Hoke get into anything like that? He could hardly bear to stand there watching Hoke. Knowing Hoke was guilty was just as bad as thinking Uncle Ed might have been.

He watched Hoke pick up the big sack of sugar, heard him grunt again as he lifted it over the doorstep. He saw Hoke step on the wooden block and go in through the doorway. There was a heavy thud as Hoke dropped the sugar on the floor inside. They listened as he went up the tiny stairway and watched as he came out again with two jars under his arm. Their eyes remained fastened on Hoke while he locked the door, and then his body blocked out their vision as he passed so close to them that Cliff could have reached out and touched his arm. As he passed by he was whistling the song about Miss Jenny.

The soft sweet sound of his whistle lingered in the air as he moved beyond them out of sight and then the melody was lost in the gentle winds that blew through the forest. The silence that fell upon them was suddenly stunning.

"It was Hoke," Ted whispered after a time. "I can't believe it."

Cliff said nothing. The shock of this terrible knowledge about Hoke left him numb as if a keg of dynamite had exploded inside of him.

For some time the boys remained motionless behind the vines, waiting. A strange sweet whistle in the distance cut through the forest silence and startled them, but it was only a bird calling out some message to his mate. Overhead, a breeze tangled the leaves and made soft rustling sounds that pricked at their straining ears.

"You think it's safe to go now?" Ted whispered to Cliff.

"I think he's gone," Cliff said. His mouth felt dry.

Ted moved cautiously out into the path. Cliff moved behind him. Stepping softly upon the spongy earth they made their way along the route they had come until they reached the big tree where the path had forked and then they turned right in the direction they had been following when Ted had discovered the second path. They crossed the little stream and had gone only a short distance when the path opened suddenly onto an old road. They stopped and looked in both directions.

"Hey, Cliff. This is the same road we were on this morning when we were riding Cricket." Ted still whispered as if afraid to speak out loud.

The great heaviness of heart that Cliff felt inside absorbed his whole mind. "I believe it is," he whispered back, hardly moving his lips, hardly knowing what he said.

"I know it is. We passed this place, where all the vines were growing, on the way to the river this morning. Remember? We said we might come back this way and go down this path." Ted motioned to Cliff. "Let's go get Cricket."

The boys began to run. They were out of breath when they reached the riverbank. Cricket was waiting. The grass was eaten short within the radius of his rope and he was standing patiently.

"Cricket," Ted said, "I know you're hot and tired." He untied the reins. "We'll have you back at home in no time flat." Ted was breathing so hard he could hardly speak.

"You reckon he can make it back home without water?" Cliff gasped, his heart pounding, fatigue and shock making him feel that his legs were made of rubber. He leaned against a tree while Ted let Cricket nibble at fresh grass. His mind was still full of what he had seen. All the fun they had enjoyed earlier had vanished.

"I guess so," Ted said. "We'll let him take it easy." His mind, too, seemed to be preoccupied for he moved restlessly about, looking off into the woods thoughtfully.

"Let's go," he said suddenly and he jumped on Cricket's back. He held the pony steady while Cliff leap-frogged over the pony's rump and settled himself behind Ted.

Cricket turned sharply and started off at a gallop. Ted tried to hold him back but the pony, eager to be back at home, raced along the path and, at the edge of the forest where the old road came out onto the river land, he turned right of his own accord toward Mr. Taylor's barnyard. Ted tried to stop him so that he could take Cliff home first but Cricket was headed for home and water and food. There was no stopping him. He did not slow down until he reached the gate. Ted got down to open it and led him in to the watering trough at the edge of the barnyard.

Cliff slid off the pony's back and for a moment stood silent beside Ted. They watched Cricket drink deeply.

There was unspoken heaviness in the air. Then Ted said, "What are you going to do, Cliff?"

"Do about what?" Cliff said, as if he did not know what Ted meant.

"About Hoke. Are we going to tell?"

"I'm not," said Cliff quickly. "I certainly don't intend to tell on Hoke." He looked at Ted defiantly as if daring Ted to challenge him.

"He's breaking the law," said Ted softly. "He's selling bootleg whiskey."

"I don't care if he is," said Cliff. "I'm not going to tell."

"You've got no right to protect him," Ted said.

Cliff bristled suddenly, feeling blood rush to his face. "What do you mean, 'I've got no right to protect him'? He's a friend of mine and I don't want to get him in trouble." He looked at Ted, seeing the pale face and tumble of blond hair with a strange wave of anger.

"He's doing something that's a crime," Ted said. "You've got no right to hide what Hoke is doing." His blue eyes were hard as ice.

Cliff's dark eyes met them with equal hardness. For a moment he did not speak as anger flooded his body.

"I don't see why you want to protect him. He's a no-good bum if he's making whiskey," Ted said.

The accumulated feelings of sorrow and shock and anger suddenly exploded into a nameless fury that shook Cliff. "You want to turn him in because he's a Negro," he said.

Ted's eyes narrowed and became little bright slits. His hands tightened into fists. "That's a black lie, Cliff."

Cliff's fists tightened, too. His teeth were clamped together. "I may be black," he hissed, "but I'm not a liar and you know it. If Hoke was a white man you wouldn't even think of telling on him."

"I didn't say you were black. I said you told a black lie when you said that, and I meant it."

Their eyes were locked in anger. The air was thick with tension.

Suddenly Mr. Taylor's voice cut through the electric moment. "Ted, where in Sam Hill have you been?"

The boys looked up as Mr. Taylor strode across the lot toward them. His long face was red and angry.

"I've got a good mind to thrash both of you," he said. "Which one of you left the pasture gate open this morning?"

Ted and Cliff looked at each other, tearing their minds away from their own anger, back to the moment they had ridden through the pasture gate on Cricket—when Cliff rode the pony through after Ted got off to open the gate.

Ted looked back at his grandfather. "I did, I guess. I didn't put the wire around the latch. We meant to go back that way."

"Well, you played hell," said Mr. Taylor. "All the mares have been out and I've chased ponies all afternoon. We still can't find Lady Red. She's out there somewhere expecting a colt any minute." He threw his hands up into the air in utter exasperation. "Get on in the house, Ted. Right this minute. Help your grandmother get supper on the table."

"What about Lady Red? I'll help you look for her," Ted said.

"I've spent the whole afternoon looking for her and I'm tired. I'm fed up with ponies and bays, too," he said. He turned away from them and walked back toward the barns.

Ted looked at Cliff. There was no warmth in his eyes. Their quarrel still hung like a heavy cloud between them and the air almost crackled with hostility.

The fact that Lady Red was lost added sharp pain to the feelings that boiled within Cliff, but did not lessen his anger at Ted. Mr. Taylor's anger only increased his own and he suddenly felt that he could stand the sight of them no longer.

Cliff turned on his heel and walked down the lane that led toward home and he never looked back.

16

SECOND THOUGHTS

The dusty road stretched out before him as Cliff strode toward his home. The setting sun behind him cast shadows that looked blood red. He welcomed the chance to walk—walk with long firm strides away from Ted and Mr. Taylor. He didn't care if he never saw them again. He was sorry about Lady Red. He felt partly responsible for leaving the gate open. It was a wonder Ted hadn't blamed that on him. His anger, hurt, and concern about Hoke throbbed painfully underneath all of this thinking, but he kept peering into the woods and up the little paths wondering if he might get a glimpse of the missing pony, at the same time fighting the waves of anger at Ted that kept sweeping over him.

He had thought Ted was a good friend. Now everything was changed. Ted wanted to tell on Hoke and he simply could not do that. Hoke had been kind to him and Hoke had helped his daddy in so many ways. He could not turn him in. Ted just didn't understand. He had said that Hoke was a no-good bum. But worse than that, Ted had called him a black liar. No. That wasn't exactly right. Ted had said he was telling a black lie. There really wasn't any difference, was there? Ted was no better than some of the white boys in his school who moved his desk last year and hid it every day so that he had to go looking for it in order to have a place to sit, or those who pushed him into any big boy he happened to be walking beside just to start a fight, or those who called him names, trying to make him feel like a nobody. He had been sure that Ted was different, but he wasn't. It was the same old stuff.

"It's not that I'm so mad at Ted," he thought. "It's just so bad to think that he's like that. I thought he was different."

He was so absorbed in his angry thoughts that he was completely surprised when a man carrying a burlap bag on his back stepped out of the woods right in front of him. It was Hoke. Panic seized Cliff.

He looked toward the woods, wishing he could hide, but Hoke had already seen him.

"Well, good afternoon," Hoke said pleasantly. "You caught me with a load of lightwood chips for starting my fires."

Cliff looked at the big burlap bag suspiciously. The bag was heavy, for Hoke was bent almost double and there were no sharp bulges such as chips might have made. The bag was full of whiskey jars and Cliff knew it. His heart began to beat furiously. "It's not chips I've caught you with," he thought. "All I have to do is whack that bag and your secret is out." He stared at Hoke with feelings of helpless shock. He didn't know how to cope with this knowledge.

"Come on and go home with me," Hoke said casually.

Cliff shook his head. Hoke knew he wouldn't go home with him. It was late and Mama would be expecting him. It was the last thing Hoke wanted—Cliff's company, and Cliff wanted to be away from Hoke, too—out of his sight.

"I'll have to get right on home," he said. "It's already getting late and Mama is expecting me."

"Well, I'll be up there tomorrow. I've been in Jackson all day. Fellow needed some help."

Cliff opened his mouth to speak, then bit his lip. Hoke was lying again. He hadn't been working for a man all day. He had been working for himself—hiding sugar in the old shack and, maybe, working at the still. Cliff remembered the smell of fresh whiskey in the bucket. He and Ted had been lucky not to run into Hoke while he was running the still. Hoke had been hiding his real activities behind excuses and lies all the time. It wasn't the first time Hoke had lied about what he was doing. Cliff wanted to confront Hoke with his knowledge. The words were on the tip of his tongue, making his heart beat harder and harder until it seemed the only sound in the whole world.

Hoke looked at him and smiled in the disarming way he had. "Not talking much today. Cat's got your tongue," he said.

Cliff felt himself grow weak. The moment for truth was gone. He simply could not say the words to Hoke.

Instead, he said, "I've got to be going. I'll see you tomorrow."

"Sure as the sun comes up," Hoke said. He crossed the lane and walked down the path toward his home, weighted down with the heavy load he carried.

Cliff watched him for a moment, bitterness and resentment filling his thoughts. "You lied to me," he said, half aloud. "Maybe you are a no-good bum." He felt betrayed by Hoke and by Ted. His whole world seemed to be breaking apart. He wanted to cry but his feeling of frustration and sorrow and hurt was too big for tears. He walked on toward home, hardly seeing the path in front of him, hardly able to focus on any logical thought, wondering only if his troubles would ever end.

He thought of Daddy. If only his daddy were at home maybe he could talk to him about some of this. "Maybe he would know what to do." But Cliff felt that telling even Daddy about Hoke would be a betrayal of friendship, somehow. No matter what Hoke had done, no matter how many lies he had told, he simply could not tell what Hoke had been doing in his spare time. And he could not tell about his quarrel with Ted because this, too, involved Hoke.

The evening was difficult and Cliff had trouble from the minute he arrived home. The little boys met him in the yard demanding to hear about his trip to the woods and whether or not he had seen the weasel. Cliff had completely forgotten about the weasel. His answers were short and he was so quiet that Mama began to question him sharply at the supper table.

"What's the matter with you, Cliff? You're not eating much supper. I thought you'd be starving after being out in the woods all day."

"Oh, we had plenty to eat," said Cliff with false cheeriness. "The sandwiches and ham and candy you packed filled me up pretty good."

"It wasn't ham she packed. It was chicken," said Paul. "I know because I helped her."

"Oh, that's right," said Cliff. "I just forgot."

Mama looked at him curiously. "I didn't really expect it to fill you up. It was hardly enough to even tease your usual appetite."

Cliff tried to smile but it was half-hearted and Mama knew it.

"If you didn't see the weasel, what did you see in the woods, Cliff?" Paul asked.

"Did you see a bear?" Wesley asked.

"Yeah," said Cliff. "A great big black bear," and as he spoke, wishing it had been a bear he had seen, he thought how similar his words were to those Ted had spoken.

"No," he said, correcting himself. "We saw a little raccoon wash his food before he ate it."

"You did?" Paul asked, his eyes shining with excitement.

"How did he do that?" Wesley asked and they listened, charmed, as Cliff forced himself to talk to them about his experiences in the woods, leaving out all the things about Hoke and the whiskey still and Ted that troubled him. He did not even tell them about Lady Red.

"But we never saw the weasel," he said finally, knowing his account had not been enthusiastic and that Mama was looking at him suspiciously.

The little boys sighed at last, satisfied with the story of his day but before he went to bed, Mama put her hand on Cliff's shoulder.

"Is everything all right, Cliff?"

He turned aside to hide the sudden sting of his eyelids and the expression he knew his eyes would reveal.

"Oh, sure," he said. "I'm just a little tired, that's all."

He pulled away from her and went to his room but he slept restlessly that night. Dreams troubled him. He kept waking up, trying to recapture what he had dreamed but the only thing he could remember was a big black bear that kept cutting him off from some place he was trying to go.

In the morning he dreaded getting up for he did not want to see Hoke again. But when he went through the day, taking care of his chores and Hoke never came at all, he felt more let down and disappointed in Hoke than before.

Hoke had told another lie and it was not the first time that Hoke had failed to show up when he was expected but now that Cliff could imagine what he was doing, he felt sick and disgusted with the knowledge. He wished a hundred times for Daddy.

"Oh, Daddy," he thought. "I know I can't tell you all that's happened, but maybe if you were here, I'd just sort of know what to do."

Mama continued to look at him with searching eyes but she said nothing. The whole day was difficult but perhaps the most disappointing thing of all was that Ted failed to come riding up the lane on Cricket. It was one of the few days that he had missed coming sometime during the day. Cliff had not really expected him, but toward dusk when he realized that Ted really was not coming, Cliff knew that he had hoped Ted would come and he faced the fact that he had missed Ted. Maybe Ted would never come again. The thought was intolerable and he began to think again of their quarrel, going over every word that had been spoken, analyzing it and wondering how it might have been different.

Maybe Ted hadn't meant to be cruel. Maybe it was wrong to accuse Ted of wanting to tell on Hoke because he was a Negro. Maybe he had been lashing out at Ted because he was worried about something else like Mama said he did with Jim when he was in the city. Maybe it was wrong to worry about Hoke—to want to protect him. Surely Hoke was a no-good bum to lie the way he did. Was it really wrong to protect him? Had Ted been right, after all?

The questions went around and around in Cliff's mind but there were no answers. One thing he did know, however. His anger at Ted was gone. The quarrel with Ted no longer seemed as important as the friendship they had enjoyed. He went to bed again—no longer bitter with anger, but with a dull heartache that was somehow even more painful to bear.

17

VISITOR AT DAWN

Cliff awoke and sat straight up in bed. Darkness pressed about him and his heart was beating rapidly. He had been dreaming. The big bear kept getting in his way and, somewhere beyond, there was a pony. He had heard the thud of pony hooves beating through his brain and a keen nicker still rang in his ears. Now there was only silence and darkness. He could not remember his dream.

He pushed his pillow to one side, flopped over on his stomach and drifted back toward sleep. He floated on the edge of his dreams with the sound of pony feet beating in rhythm with his heart and then he heard the sound once more—the high shrill nicker. He sat up in bed again.

That sounded like Cricket! He leaped out of bed and

went to his side window. The first pale streaks of dawn lighted the sky in the east and objects were dimly outlined against it. He saw movement close to the fence beside his window.

"Cricket," he said softly. There was an answering whinny.

He was right. It was Cricket. What was he doing here at this house at this time of the morning? Cliff turned on his light and looked at his clock. It was five o'clock. In another thirty minutes it would be light.

Cliff slipped into his trousers and a T-shirt. He went across the hall and opened the porch door softly. Then he ran to the back door and down the steps. He heard the pony's hoof hit against the plank fence.

"I'm coming, Cricket," he called softly. The pony snorted.

Cliff let himself through the gate and Cricket ran up to him as he went through it. The pony stood quietly while Cliff patted his neck and ran his hands along the pony's sides. There seemed to be nothing wrong with the pony except that he was hot. He had been running. Why? Why was he here? Why had he come here at this hour?

"He might have broken out of the pasture," Cliff thought, and then he knew that this was wrong. Cricket was wearing a bridle. Someone had been riding him and that someone had to be Ted.

"What's the matter, Cricket?" he asked softly. "What are you doing here? Where's Ted?"

The pony's head jerked up and he pawed at the earth. Cliff stood thinking for a moment. Something was wrong. Ted had certainly been riding him. But he would not have left Cricket with the bridle on unless . . . There Cliff's thought came to a dead end. Should he take the pony back to Mr. Taylor? What would he find there? Would

Mr. Taylor be angry? Would Ted still be mad? Cliff felt
a strong sense of foreboding rising within him as he stood
trying to decide what to do.

He looked at the sky. Already he could distinguish
objects. Mr. Taylor's household would be up shortly.
Somebody had to take the pony back. Something was
surely wrong and Mr. Taylor might not even know about
it. In that moment Cliff knew that he would be com-
pelled to find out what was wrong. Some sense of urgency
told him that he must act quickly and his thoughts of
alarm were focused upon Ted.

He hesitated for an instant wondering if he should tell
Mama where he was going but the house was quiet. Mama
was still sleeping and he would certainly be back before
she woke up. She would not even know that he was gone.

He jumped lightly onto Cricket's back and before he
could settle himself, Cricket was off with a rattle of hoofbeats. He turned the corner in front of the house and
they passed Daddy's station wagon parked close beside
the front gate.

"Daddy's home," Cliff thought. "He must have come
in late last night after I went to sleep. Maybe I should
call him." The thought flashed through his mind but
there was no stopping Cricket. The pony was galloping
full speed toward Mr. Taylor's home. Cliff did not see the
light come on in his parents' room.

They raced past Hoke's house where Cliff could see a
light. Smoke was already curling from the chimney. "He's
probably been out working at his still all night," Cliff
thought bitterly, but he was glad there was no sign of
him outside. Cricket ran on.

Suddenly the pony slowed his pace and when they
reached the old woods road he turned in.

"Whoa, Cricket. Where are you going?" Cliff asked in

alarm. He had no desire to go down into the woods which were deeply shadowed. He thought of Hoke who was already up and perhaps, even now, was at his still. He pulled the pony to a halt and turned him around. "We're going to Ted's house, now. We can't go exploring this early in the morning."

The pony broke into a run again. He ran along the lane until he drew up panting beside the Taylor farmhouse. Lights were on in the kitchen, and Mr. Taylor came outside so quickly that it seemed as if he had been waiting for Cliff. His manner was sharp and anxious.

"Cliff. Where'd you come from?" he asked. "I was just getting ready to go to your house." He looked worried and Cliff jumped off the pony quickly.

"I came from home, Mr. Taylor."

"Where's Ted? Where did you find Cricket?"

"I don't know where Ted is. I thought he was here. Cricket was outside my window when I woke up and I thought you'd want him back. Isn't Ted here?"

"No. He's not and we're mighty worried. Ted hasn't been here since yesterday evening. He went off on Cricket and he didn't come back last night." Mr. Taylor opened the gate and Cliff led the pony inside and waited while Mr. Taylor looked him over.

"We rode everywhere looking for him when he didn't come home by nine o'clock. We knew he was out on Cricket and we kept hoping he'd show up."

"Did he say anything when he left about where he was going?" Cliff asked.

"No. He was worried and he kept talking about Lady Red."

"Then you haven't found her yet?" Cliff asked.

"Not a sign of her. We think Ted went looking for her. I was pretty upset about her and he knew that."

"I'm sorry about her, too, Mr. Taylor," said Cliff.

"Well, she's not so important now," said Mr. Taylor. "I'm just concerned about that boy. I was hoping maybe you might know where he would have gone."

Mrs. Taylor had come out onto the porch. She had been crying and she kept brushing her hair back away from her face nervously as she listened to them talk.

"You don't have any idea where Ted might be, do you?" she asked, her voice quavering slightly.

"No, ma'am," Cliff said, and then a thought occurred to him. Cricket had turned in at the old woods path. Could that be where Ted had gone?

"No, ma'am," he said again. "I'm not sure, but I have an idea I might know which way he went."

"I'm sure he's been hurt," said Mrs. Taylor. "He would have been back if he could have gotten here. And now that Cricket's come up, I'm just sure of it." She twisted her hands together and her voice broke altogether.

"We'd be mighty thankful if you could help us," Mr. Taylor said. "We've already called the sheriff to come help us find him. I'm expecting him any minute. He said he'd be here as soon as it was light enough to see."

"Ted's folks will be so upset. We haven't called them yet," said Mrs. Taylor.

"I'm not sure I can find him, but I do have an idea where to look," Cliff said. The thought that he might run into Hoke if he went down into the woods crossed his mind and the idea frightened him. He pushed his fear deep within him. He'd have to face that when he came to it.

"Would it be a good idea for me to go with you?" Mr. Taylor asked.

Cliff thought a moment. He weighed his fear of meeting Hoke against the strange and fiercely protective feeling he had toward Hoke. Then he shook his head. "No," he said quickly. "I don't mind going. You might want to wait for the sheriff. I'll just take Cricket. I think he knows exactly where to go."

He jumped on Cricket's back and before Mr. Taylor could say another word they had turned sharply away from him and were out through the gate, racing back toward the woods path that Cliff was now sure Ted had taken to look for Lady Red.

18

TO TELL OR NOT TO TELL

Cliff's thoughts were flying ahead of Cricket's feet. He tried to put himself in Ted's shoes and think the way Ted might have been thinking yesterday afternoon.

Ted was worried because his grandfather was upset over Lady Red. He was desperate to find her. He tried to think which way the mare might have walked. If she had gone down into the woods she would have had to drink water. The first place Ted would have thought of would have been the pond. But how would Lady Red have gotten there? Which way would she have gone?

Cliff thought of the little path beyond the whiskey still and the way it ran along the stream.

"If that's the path animals follow, Lady Red might have gone that way," he thought, but he was uncertain that the pony could have gotten through the vines on the far side of the area around the still.

She could have gone on closer to the river. "That way she might have gotten around that thick patch of vines," he thought. The more he reasoned it out, the more certain he was that his search would lead him to the pond.

But which was the best way to go?

The sun appeared above the east horizon just as Cricket turned in at the old woods road. He trotted along the path between the tall trees.

"I could get off and walk," Cliff thought, "but I can't go by the whiskey still. Hoke might be there." The thought of meeting Hoke at the whiskey still sent a chill down Cliff's spine and this troubled him. He didn't want to be afraid of Hoke. He wasn't even sure that he was afraid. Yet, his feeling for Hoke had changed in some way and he wanted to take no chance of running into him.

"I'll have to go down to the river and walk toward the pond that way," he decided.

He nudged Cricket on as they approached the tangle of vines behind which lay the old shack and the whiskey still, but Cricket stopped suddenly. He backed up a few steps and than pranced on nervous feet up and down the rutted path.

"What is it, Cricket? What's the matter? Are you afraid?" Cliff looked nervously down at the path ahead to see if something had frightened the pony, a snake or an animal, but there was nothing.

Cricket stood quite still. He whinnied. A deep silence followed and then Cliff heard a sound. Cricket's ears pricked forward and he whinnied again. Cliff listened.

He heard the sound again. Someone was calling faintly. "Cricket." The voice was Ted's! He was somewhere behind those vines.

Cliff felt an electric tingle go through his body. Was Ted hurt? Tied up so he couldn't get away? Was Hoke in there? Should he turn back for help now?

"Cricket." The voice came more faintly now and ended with a groan.

Cliff dropped from Cricket's back. Ted was in real trouble. He had to find out what it was. He couldn't take time to go back for help without knowing what had happened to Ted. He ignored the waves of fear that swept over him as he left Cricket standing in the path and walked down the half-concealed path in the direction of Ted's voice. Where the path separated at the poplar tree, he hesitated. Then, instinct took him toward the whiskey still.

He slipped silently between the layers of vines and stepped out into the opening, almost stumbling over Lady Red who lay prone upon the vine-covered earth, breathing heavily.

Beside her stood a little stud foal, a bright sorrel image of his mother. His saucy white tail twitched once and he regarded Cliff with large curious eyes. Cliff's heart leaped at the sight of the beautiful little pony but his eyes were searching for Ted and they swept over the area.

He saw Ted then, lying close to the stream that ran through the area. Ted lay quite still on his back with both arms thrown up over his eyes.

For a brief moment, Cliff looked at Ted anxiously. He knew that Ted was hurt but he had the curious feeling that Ted was in another world and he hesitated to intrude upon this privacy of pain. He felt an urgent impulse to run toward Ted, yet he moved toward him slowly and spoke softly.

"Ted." Cliff was standing over Ted.

Ted moved his arms away from his face and opened his eyes. At first he stared wildly into space above him as if his eyes could not focus and then he turned his head and looked at Cliff. His pale face was swollen and covered with red mosquito bites. His arms, too, were peppered with bites, and several mosquitos flew up as he moved his hand.

"Cliff," he said weakly. "Oh, Cliff. Am I glad—to see you." He began to cry. "I dreamed—I heard Cricket."

Cliff knelt beside him and put his hand on Ted's shoulder.

"You did hear Cricket," he said, "and it's a good thing you did. I heard you call him." He wished for a handkerchief to wipe Ted's spotted face.

"Are you hurt?"

"It's my leg," Ted said. He tried to pull himself up on one arm but he fell back with a groan. "I think—it's broken." His voice was so weak it was hardly possible to understand the words.

Cliff looked quickly down at Ted's leg. The shoe and sock had been removed and Cliff could see that the foot was twisted at an angle. The skin, two inches above the ankle, was blue and something protruded beneath the skin.

"It sure looks funny," he said. "I think it must be broken, but the bone hasn't come through the skin."

Ted groaned. "I thought—nobody would find me. I stumbled—in a hole. I've been trying to crawl out—but I can't."

Cliff stared at Ted with a sense of distracted concern. Ted needed help quickly. He looked around him and realized with a sudden flood of relief that Hoke was not anywhere about. He looked back at Ted. He had to get Ted home somehow.

"I've got Cricket out there," he said. "Do you think you can stand up on one leg if I help you?"

"I'll try," said Ted weakly.

"Wait," said Cliff. He ran past Lady Red and the little foal and through the vines along the path to where Cricket stood waiting. He led the pony back across the small stream and into the vine-covered area.

Lady Red, still breathing with great difficulty, had not moved. She seemed unaware of anything around her. The foal moved away from her for the first time. He walked on wobbly legs toward Cricket and nuzzled him as if looking for a place to nurse. Cricket shied away.

"Be still," Cliff said sharply to Cricket, trying to guide him close to Ted. The little foal darted away and walked unsteadily back to his mother's side.

Cliff knelt beside Ted and slipped his sturdy arms beneath Ted's shoulders. He lifted gently but Ted screamed in an agony of pain.

"I can't stand it," he cried. Tears flooded his eyes and spilled over his swollen cheeks. He wiped them away with one bare arm, red and swollen with bites. Then he lay quiet with his eyes closed as if he had drifted off into another world.

Cliff stood up and stared down at Ted helplessly. He began to wring his hands and then looked frantically about him.

"Maybe I could make a splint," he said to Ted but Ted did not seem to notice his words. Cliff stood hesitant with indecision. He was afraid to touch Ted for fear he would hurt him again. There was nothing he could do alone. He had to go for help.

"Listen, Ted," he said, kneeling again. Ted's eyes were still closed. "Listen to me. I'm going for help. I'll be back as quick as I can. Don't try to move."

If Ted heard him, he gave no indication and Cliff jumped to his feet in panic. Ted did not seem to be conscious. He had to get help quickly. He led Cricket back toward the old road and, once there, he mounted the pony with one quick leap.

"Let's go, Cricket," he commanded. "Ted's got to have help."

He was halfway out of the woods when he realized with sudden dismay that to get help for Ted would expose Hoke's secret. The thought swept over him in a hot wave of distress that made him feel shaky inside. No matter what Hoke had done, he did not want to tell on him.

"But I've got no choice," he thought with almost a sob. "I've just got no other choice. We've got to get Ted out of there. I've got to tell. I've absolutely got to tell." The thought beat itself out inside his brain as if in rhythm with Cricket's hoofbeats.

At the edge of the woods, however, Cliff jerked the reins hard and sharply. Cricket drew to a complete halt and stood panting. For a moment Cliff remained motionless on the pony, deep in thought.

With sudden resolution, he pulled the left rein and turned the pony in the direction opposite that which would take him to Mr. Taylor's house. He raced down the path along the woods. Two hundred yards farther he stopped short before Hoke's front door and he called loudly.

"Hoke."

Hoke appeared almost instantly, fully clothed. He had an open carton of milk in his hand as if he were just ready to pour out some for his breakfast.

"Well, hello, there. You're out early this morning," Hoke said cheerfully.

Cliff swallowed once and then he said, "Hoke, Ted's hurt and he's down there in the woods. I've got to go for help and I wanted you to know I'll have to tell about what you've been doing."

Hoke's face looked blank and innocent. "What in the world are you talking about, Cliff?"

"You know what I'm talking about. It's your whiskey still and they'll find it when they go to get Ted. Lady Red's in there, too, with her colt. She's sick, too, and the doctor will be needed. I just wanted you to know. I hate to tell where they are but I've got no choice. Ted's hurt bad and he's been out there in the woods all night. The sheriff's coming down here."

He could see no change of expression in Hoke's pleasant face and before Hoke could speak Cliff turned the pony around and gave him a quick kick. Cricket was off again with a flash of heels beating on the dusty path.

"Hurry, hurry, Cricket. We've used up some of our time and we've got to get to Mr. Taylor," he said. "I don't know what Hoke will do now. He may run away, but I had to tell him. I just simply had to."

19

RESCUE

Even before Cliff reached Mr. Taylor's house he saw the station wagon and his heart beat a degree lighter.

"Daddy's there," he thought as he raced forward.

There were other cars there, too, and when he pulled Cricket to a halt at the gate to the yard where a group of men and Mrs. Taylor were gathered he realized that the sheriff and his deputies had already arrived. All eyes were fastened on him.

"I've found him, Mr. Taylor," he called out and then he jumped off the pony. "He's in the woods."

"Thank God," said Mrs. Taylor pushing her hair back from her face which was still red and swollen from crying.

"Is he all right?" Mr. Taylor asked.

"No, sir. I wouldn't say that. He's hurt. I think his leg is broken. The bone looks like it's sticking up and he's in awful pain. You ought to get there as quick as you can," he added. "Lady Red's there, too, and she's had her colt but she looks mighty sick."

Mr. Taylor nodded as if this were an unimportant matter.

"Come on," said the sheriff. "Show us where he is." He was a heavy well-built man with eyes that looked at Cliff keenly.

"Would you like to take the station wagon?" Daddy asked. "You might like to stretch Ted out in the back."

"That's fine," said Mr. Taylor. "We'll have to get him to a hospital if his leg is broken. I'll ride with you."

Cliff tied Cricket to the fence and hopped in the sheriff's car beside Sheriff Kimball. Two of his deputies got in the back seat and another one climbed in the station wagon with Daddy and Mr. Taylor.

They lost no time getting to the woods path and here Sheriff Kimball turned in.

"Can we make it down this path, Cliff?" he asked.

"I think so," said Cliff. "There are lots of ruts but no real bad holes. Cricket just flies along here now."

They bumped along over the ruts with limbs of underbrush hitting the windows of the car until they reached the thick vines.

"Stop here," Cliff said.

The sheriff stopped and the men got out quickly. Daddy's station wagon was right behind them. Cliff's heart was beating hard against his chest. Would Ted be all right? Was Hoke in there with him? Had he done right to let Hoke know? Was the little pony still there? Would Lady Red be all right? Questions boiled inside his mind.

He walked quickly along the little path which had become so familiar to him. He stepped inside the secluded area and walked around Lady Red. She was no longer breathing and the little pony lay close beside her. He lifted his head as Cliff walked by him but he did not get up. Cliff's eyes moved quickly across the area toward Ted. Hoke was there, kneeling beside Ted, fanning him with the milk carton which he had ripped apart and spread out. Ted's eyes were closed.

Hoke looked up at the men as they filed into the area and then he stood up and moved aside while Mr. Taylor hurried in with hardly a glance at the pony and her colt. He knelt beside his grandson.

"Ted," Mr. Taylor said.

Ted opened his eyes.

"Granddaddy," he said. Tears began to roll from his eyes down the side of his face. Mr. Taylor took out his handkerchief and wiped the swollen tear-stained face.

"It's all right, Ted. You're going to be all right now."

"Cliff—he knew—where—"

"He knew where to look for you. I know," said Mr. Taylor.

"Can we get him up?" asked the sherriff.

"We need a splint on this leg so we can move him," said Mr. Taylor.

"I've got some bandage in my station wagon," said Daddy. "If we can find a straight stick, I think we'll have all we need to work it out." He went back to the station wagon.

Ted tried to lift his head but it fell back weakly. "Lady Red—" he said. "She died—I'm so—sorry."

"It's all right, Ted," said Mr. Taylor. "You stop worrying about that."

"The foal—he's getting—weak."

"I know," said Mr. Taylor. "We'll work on him later when we get you squared away."

"Lady Red—was tumbling around," said Ted. His words came in painful snatches between gasps of breath. "She pushed—me—backward. My foot got caught—stump hole—over there." He motioned feebly toward the little stream along the side of the open area.

"Don't worry," said Mr. Taylor. "Just don't try to talk. We'll have you out of here in five minutes. We'll stretch you out in Mr. Morgan's station wagon and take you where they'll make you more comfortable."

Ted closed his eyes and Cliff walked over in the direction Ted had indicated. Beside the stream there was a hole where the stump of a pine tree had rotted away. This must have been where Ted's ankle got caught.

Daddy came back with the box of wide bandage and took the stick that Sheriff Kimball handed to him. He knelt beside Mr. Taylor and his gentle hands began to strap the broken ankle to the stick. Ted moaned in pain while Mr. Taylor held his hand and stroked his head, uttering comforting and encouraging words. Cliff turned away, unable to bear the pain that Ted was suffering.

It was then that he saw the three deputies bending over the barrels of mash. Sheriff Kimball had joined them as they looked.

"Looks like Ted stumbled over more than a stump hole," said one of the deputies to the sheriff.

"Seems so," said Sheriff Kimball. "Wonder whose it is?" He looked directly at Cliff. "You knew exactly where to find Ted. You've been here before. What do you know about it, Cliff?"

There was a sudden deafening silence in the open

area as if time stood still and all sounds in the world had
ceased.

In spite of a supreme effort to keep his eyes fastened
on Sheriff Kimball, they swept over the area and rested
for an instant on Hoke who was bending over the little
foal. Hoke looked up and their eyes met. Hoke's eyes were
filled with just a shadow of amusement mixed with a sort
of rueful sorrow. Cliff's own eyes were touched with dismay and anxiety that he felt for Ted and for Hoke, too.
Blood rushed to his face. His heart was pounding furiously.
He opened his mouth to speak but the words just would
not come. He clamped his teeth together tightly, and his
eyes dropped.

"Speak up, Cliff. Tell me what you know," Sheriff Kimball said.

In the silence that followed he heard Hoke laugh shortly.
"The boy's in a spot, Sheriff. The still belongs to me." His
mellow voice fell upon Cliff's ears like claps of thunder,
but with them Cliff felt suddenly lighter, as if a weight
of great magnitude had slipped from his shoulders.

He looked again at Hoke, his expression reflecting both
the relief that he felt and a new anxiety about what would
happen to Hoke now that he had confessed that the still
was his. There were so many mixed feelings inside that
he could never express. He wished he could talk to Hoke
but he didn't know what he could say. Besides, there were
too many people around.

Cliff turned to face Sheriff Kimball, "What does this
mean, Sheriff? What will you do to him?"

"That all depends on Hoke and his attitude," said the
sheriff. "If he tries to run away, it might be pretty tough
on him."

Cliff looked straight into the sheriff's keen eyes. "He had a chance to run away. He knew you would be here to help find Ted."

Hoke laughed again, shortly, without much humor. "That's right, Sheriff. If I had planned to run, I wouldn't be here now. I'd have been long gone before you got here."

"How did you know we'd be here?" the sheriff asked.

Cliff spoke before Hoke could answer. "I told him," he said. "I told him Ted was down here hurt and he came to see if he could help Ted."

At that moment Ted groaned loudly and they all turned toward Mr. Taylor who was lifting his grandson. Daddy hurried ahead of Mr. Taylor to open the back of the station wagon. Ted was crying, his face twisted in a grimace of pain. The men beat back a wider path between the vines so they could get Ted through and Cliff ran ahead to help Daddy clear away the supplies that were stored in the back of the station wagon.

Mrs. Taylor had given them a quilt which they spread on the bottom of the floor and another to wrap him in. Cliff watched Daddy and Mr. Taylor lift Ted gently onto the quilt. He jumped inside to move a box farther away from Ted's head. The sight of Ted's swollen face, speckled with red mosquito bites, stained with tears, and altered by pain filled him with an aching misery. He wanted to ease Ted's pain in some way. He took off his shirt and folded it to place beneath Ted's head.

Ted opened his eyes and looked up at him. His mouth twisted in a feeble grin.

"Cliff," he said. "I never meant—what—you thought I did. I wouldn't—have—I couldn't sleep—thinking about it. You've—been great—all summer."

Cliff felt his eyelids sting and his throat filled up with a big lump. "It's okay, Ted. I had a chip on my shoulder that I wanted you to knock off."

Ted winced with pain as Mr. Taylor adjusted him in a better position for his ride to the hospital and placed the folded shirt under Ted's cheek. "You were—the—only one—You were—" Ted tried to say something more to Cliff, but his voice trailed off and he closed his eyes.

"He still wants to say you were the only one who knew where to look for him," said Mr. Taylor to Cliff. "And I'm mighty thankful, too."

Daddy was in the front seat ready to start the station wagon.

"I guess we'll go by and pick up Mrs. Taylor. She'll want to go to the hospital with us," Mr. Taylor told Daddy.

At that moment Hoke called out from the edge of the vines.

"What about the little foal, Mr. Taylor? What do you want to do with him?"

"Give him to Cliff," said Mr. Taylor.

Cliff jumped out of the back end of the station wagon. "Yes, sir. I'll look after him until you get back," he said.

"No. You keep him, Cliff. He's yours if you can make him live. A colt without his mother is the last thing on earth I want to worry about now. Let's go," he said to Daddy.

Cliff watched the station wagon back down the path. His knees were weak. So much had happened. But Ted was going to be all right. And the little colt—Did Mr. Taylor really say he could have it?

The full realization hit him with sudden stunning impact. A tingle of pure joy swept through him. The colt was his. He could not believe it. But it was true. Mr. Taylor had spoken the words.

He turned to run back toward the open area where the colt lay beside his mother and there was Hoke walking out from the wall of vines with the little foal in his arms. Sheriff Kimball was behind him.

"Cliff," said Sheriff Kimball. "I'm letting Hoke take the little colt home for you. He's on his honor to wait there for me until we can pick him up. I'm sort of putting him in your care."

Cliff nodded but he felt uncomfortable.

"You don't have to worry about me, Sheriff," said Hoke. He cradled the foal in his arms like a baby. "Come on, Cliff. This little thing is hungry and weak. We've got to get some food in him."

They started walking away from the sheriff and Cliff heard crashing sounds behind the vines.

"What are they doing?" he asked Hoke.

Hoke did not speak for a few moments as they walked down the rutted path. Then he said, "They're breaking up my easy-money machine." He laughed, but it was not the easy free laughter Cliff usually heard from Hoke.

"Easy-money machine?"

"That's what I called it," said Hoke. "But the money I have to pay in fines won't come so easy. You boys broke up a beautiful operation."

"I'm really sorry about all of this, Hoke. I didn't want to be the one to tell—"

"You didn't tell, Cliff. You were caught just like I was and there was no choice. But I always say if you want to dance to the music, you have to pay the fiddler."

"But you did have a choice, Hoke. You had time to get away. You could have gone."

"No, Cliff. When you run away from something you have to keep on running. That's just too much trouble. Besides, I thought about the boy, down there hurt and I know how bad the mosquitoes are. I didn't know how long it would take Mr. Taylor to get there. I didn't have much choice."

They turned out of the woods path onto the lane toward Cliff's home. The silence between them seemed as big as all outdoors. Cliff's feelings about Hoke were confused. Hoke had made a choice because he was worried about Ted, but he had been wrong about so many things. Cliff felt more and more uncomfortable and he did not know what to say to Hoke. But one question bubbled forth from his deep concern.

"What will they do to you, Hoke?"

"Let's don't talk about that, Cliff. Let's get Lady Red's baby home. Did I ever tell you the story about the raccoon and the mule?"

Cliff stared at Hoke with a measure of contempt. He couldn't understand Hoke's light offhand manner. This was a mighty poor time for a story. He didn't want to hear any story. He couldn't bear to have Hoke talk about foolish things at a time like this—not when he felt anxious about Ted and about the pony whose head was dangling from Hoke's arms as if it were dying.

He walked on toward home and breakfast and Mama, wondering how she would feel about the pitiful little foal, hardly hearing Hoke's words as he told about the raccoon and the mule.

20

LADY RED'S BABY

It was late in the afternoon. The little pony lay stretched out on the porch and Cliff sat beside him holding a bottle which contained two ounces of milk made up according to a formula that Dr. Harrington had given Mama when she telephoned him that morning after Hoke had left with the sheriff.

Mama came out onto the back porch and sat down on the floor beside Cliff, crossing her slim brown legs under her. She was wearing dark Bermudas and a bright red sleeveless blouse. Her dark hair was pulled to the crown of her head where it fell in a tumble of crisp curls. It was hard to believe she had finished all her housework, cooked two meals, finished the dishes and the washing. Mama had a way of looking cool and fresh no matter how much work she had done.

"Now, I can help you again, Cliff," she said. "Want me to hold his head?"

"Let me hold the bottle a little while, Cliff," said Paul. He was sitting as close to the foal as he could get without touching him.

"Me, too," said Wesley, holding out his fat little hand.

Cliff shook his head and looked at Mama beseechingly. "Tell them, Mama. I can't make them understand."

"Paul, honey, the little colt is still so weak we have to be sure he's fed just right. Cliff's afraid if you jiggle the bottle, the milk might go down the wrong way and he'd get choked. We just don't want that to happen."

"I promise not to jiggle. I'll hold it straight and still," Paul said.

Mama pulled Paul over into her lap and hugged him. "If the little pony gets strong enough to stand up again, you can certainly hold the bottle. And Wesley can, too."

"Dr. Harrington said we should feed him every two hours, Paul," said Cliff, "so there'll be plenty of time to feed him if we can only pull him through the next few hours. We've got to get him back on his feet."

"What made him get so weak?"

"His mama was sick such a long time and he couldn't nurse her," Cliff said.

"Tell us again how he tried to nurse Cricket when you were in the woods," Paul said.

"He was just so hungry he was looking for food anywhere he thought he might find some. Cricket looked like the best place to hunt. Hoke said he would not have come close to us if he hadn't been so hungry."

"What are you going to name him, Cliff?"

"I don't really know," said Cliff. "I haven't had time to think about it yet."

Mama held the pony's head up while Cliff pushed the long nipple in between the velvet-soft lips. The little muzzle wrinkled and the nipple slipped from his mouth.

"Put some of the milk on the outside of the nipple, Cliff," Mama suggested.

Cliff snapped the nipple off and wet it with milk. Then he replaced the nipple and inserted it in the pony's mouth again. This time he grasped it and began to suck.

"Look. I think he's drinking better this time," Paul said.

Wesley leaned over Paul to get a better look. As he did, the little foal pushed his tongue against the nipple and milk dripped out the side of his mouth.

"I don't think it's really going down," Cliff said.

"It's hard to tell how much he's getting," said Mama. "He's certainly losing some."

"If Daddy ever gets back, maybe he will know how to get more into him," Cliff said. He was beginning to feel discouraged.

"Maybe so," said Mama. "Daddy should be back before too long. We'll just have to keep on like this until he comes. Dr. Harrington said we should be careful not to let him get strangled. I don't see how we could do it differently." She turned the pony's head so the milk might go down more directly. The pony tried to suck again.

"Rub his throat, Mama," Cliff said. "That's the way Dr. Harrington did when he poured the medicine down Fast Buck's throat."

Mama stroked the pony's neck but he jerked his head away so that the nipple slipped out again. Milk streamed from his mouth down toward his throat latch.

"Oh, dear," Mama said. "That doesn't seem to work either."

Cliff put the nipple back into the pony's mouth and again the foal sucked. This time he swallowed several times.

"Some went down that time," Cliff said.

"He wants to drink but somehow he just hasn't got the hang of drinking from a bottle," Mama said.

They heard a footstep on the front porch and then the front screen door slammed.

"It's Daddy," Paul said. He and Wesley stood up just as Daddy came out onto the back porch. At the same time, Mr. Taylor's car came to a stop beside the back gate.

"It's Mr. Taylor," Cliff said.

"He wanted to drive down here and see how the pony's doing," Daddy said.

"How is Ted?" Cliff said, eager to hear.

"He's going to be all right," said Daddy opening the back screen door for Mr. Taylor who walked across the yard and came up the steps. Mama laid the pony's head gently on the floor and stood up.

"We're so glad that Ted's going to be all right," she said to Mr. Taylor as he joined them.

"Yes, I think he'll be fine in a few days—thanks to you, Cliff. We all feel mighty grateful. I'm sure we might not have found him so soon if you hadn't known where to look, and his leg might have given him serious trouble if he had gone much longer without attention."

"Was the break a bad one?" Mama wanted to know.

"It was about as bad as one can be without breaking the skin. He was suffering from shock and mosquito bites, too. They almost ate him up."

"Is he still in pain?" Cliff asked.

"They put him to sleep to set the bone and put on a cast. Then they gave him something to keep him asleep for awhile," said Mr. Taylor. "He asked me to bring you back over when he's well enough to see you."

Cliff smiled, his eyes lighting up with pleasure. "I'd certainly like to go."

"We'll make arrangements to take you. His grandmother is staying with him until his mother and father get here from Raleigh. I expect they'll take him back to Raleigh with them as soon as he's able to travel."

"I'll surely miss him," Cliff said, thinking of how lonely it would be without seeing Ted every day, riding, talking, having adventures together. He thought then of Lady Red.

"I'm mighty sorry about your pony, about Lady Red. I know how much you thought of her."

"Well, yes. I did think a lot of her and I was sorry to lose her."

"I didn't really understand why she got so sick," said. Cliff.

"She ate the sour mash at the whiskey still, Cliff. That's crushed grain you know. She probably ate some of the molded rye grain that was on the ground, too. That would have given her encephalitis which is a brain disease even if she had not died from eating the mash."

"Did eating that cause something like eating wet peanut vines causes?" Cliff asked.

"Something like that. The mash formed gas and in this case it ruptured the intestine. She died of peritonitis. She didn't have a chance."

Cliff shook his head. "What will you do about her? Will you just leave her out there in the woods?"

"I've arranged to have her buried out there where she died," said Mr. Taylor. "Oh, and that reminds me. I have something to show you that Sheriff Kimball found when they were breaking up the still."

He left the porch, went back to his car, got something from the floor of the back seat while Cliff waited on the porch with his family. He was completely mystified. But even before Mr. Taylor walked back up the steps, Cliff saw what it was. The steel trap!

Mr. Taylor laid it on the floor and Cliff bent to look. Mama and the boys looked, too. Caught between its teeth was a tiny paw, ragged and dark with dried blood. Cliff looked up at Mr. Taylor and then at Daddy as the full implication of the tiny paw struck him.

"The weasel chewed off his foot, didn't he?"

Daddy nodded. "That's right. We thought you'd be interested in seeing it."

"How about that!" said Cliff in amazement. "He's free again."

"That's one way to look at it," Daddy said.

"That's one way to get rid of a burden," said Mr. Taylor.

"But he's only got three legs now," said little Paul.

"That's right, Paul, but he's free," said Cliff and the thought brought a little smile to his lips.

"The sheriff brought it by the house before he left," said Mr. Taylor. "We figured since weasels eat garbage, he might have been after the same mash that killed Lady Red."

Cliff's thoughts returned to Lady Red. "I'm really sorry we caused so much trouble, Mr. Taylor. I felt it was all our fault because we didn't go back and fasten the gate with the wire."

"Well, I should have had a better way of fastening the gate. A lot of things can happen when you're raising ponies, as you know. But that's part of the pony business, I guess—and part of the boy business, too. But I don't want to give up either one—ponies or boys. Matter of fact, I may need you to help me take these ponies to the sale next week, if your daddy can spare you—now that Ted's out of commission."

"Oh, yes. Yes, sir," said Cliff. "I'd like that a lot."

Daddy nodded when Cliff looked at him. "Mr. Taylor and I have already talked about it," he said. "I'll be home from now on and I guess I can let you get away for a day."

Cliff's eyes were shining with pleasure over this new prospect.

"What about this little fellow?" Mr. Taylor asked. "How's he doing?"

"I'm afraid he's getting weaker," Cliff said. "We're having a hard time getting the milk in him and he won't stand up anymore."

"Let's see what we can do," Mr. Taylor said. He laid his hat on a chair beside the door and then leaned down. He lifted the pony to his feet. The little creature's legs wobbled under him and when Mr. Taylor turned him loose, they buckled as if he would fall. Mr. Taylor's large hands caught him.

"He's just got to have milk," he said. "What are you giving him?"

"We mixed a formula," Mama said. "Dr. Harrington gave it to us over the telephone. It's twenty ounces of milk, twelve ounces of lime water, and four tablespoons of sugar. We're supposed to give him two ounces every two hours."

"That's fine," said Mr. Taylor. "Although, you may have to make it every hour until you are sure he's getting all you give him and he gets a little stronger."

He stood up and straddled the little foal, holding his head between his hands. "Here, Cliff. You put the bottle in his mouth while I hold him in this standing position. This way his throat stretches out like it does when he nurses his mother."

Cliff put the nipple in the pony's mouth and he sucked weakly. Cliff saw his throat contract several times.

"He's swallowing," he said with delight. "It's really going down." He held the bottle until the last drop was gone.

Mr. Taylor turned him loose and the pony folded up and stretched out on the floor.

Mr. Taylor shook his head. "I don't know whether he'll make it or not. That's why I don't want the trouble of fooling with him. I've got too much to do. I haven't had much luck trying to raise them on a bottle. It just takes too much patience."

"It can be done, can't it?" Cliff asked anxiously.

"Let's put it this way, Cliff. It has been done. You keep giving him an ounce of milk every hour through the night. If he gets so he'll stand up by himself, you can know you've got it made. Then you can feed him two ounces every two hours. He's really a nice one—worth saving."

Cliff smiled a little and pressed his lips together. "If patience is what it takes, I'll find some extra around here."

"He's not kidding about that," Daddy said to Mr. Taylor who picked up his hat.

"Let me know if I can help you," Mr. Taylor said as he was leaving.

"Let us know how Ted gets along," said Mama. "We'll be anxious to hear from him."

Cliff had already gone into the kitchen to wash out the bottle so it would be ready for the next feeding.

21

SUNRISE IN OCCONEECHEE

They ate supper in the kitchen between feedings. At times Cliff felt encouraged. Once or twice the pony lifted his head when he was lying down between feedings and sometimes he pulled at the bottle as if impatient, but most of the time he lay lifeless on the floor of the porch which Mama had covered with newspapers and some old burlap bags.

All through the night Cliff kept watch with Mama and Daddy helping. Occasionally, Daddy would go into the living room and get a few minutes of sleep in his big chair, but he was always there when the time for feeding came.

It was after midnight when he and Cliff were sitting

together on the porch and Mama was taking a nap in her bedroom. The cool moist night air blew gently across them as they sat at the big table. Cliff was tired. His body felt weighted down with anxious thoughts about the foal. His arms sometimes felt too weak to hold the bottle. His mind seemed hazy as it wandered over the events of the day. He thought of Hoke.

"Daddy, what do you think they'll do to Hoke?"

"There are several things they can do to him," Daddy said. His voice was quiet and gentle in the dim light they had on the porch. "Ordinarily he might be sentenced to one or two years in prison, but this is his first offense and the fact that he turned himself in might convince the judge that his sentence should be suspended."

"What does that mean?"

"It means that he will not actually have to serve any time in prison. He may get off with paying a fine."

"That's what Hoke meant by having to work to pay for what he's done. Will that be much?"

"It could be two or three hundred dollars. Enough to make him sweat, but it won't ruin him."

"I didn't want to see him get in trouble," said Cliff. "That's why I didn't want to tell about him."

"How did you know about it, Cliff?"

"Ted and I were down there in the woods. We found the still and then we saw Hoke when he brought some sugar down to the old shack that's nearby. There's lots of whiskey in there."

"Sheriff Kimball and his men found that, too," said Daddy. "They confiscated the still and poured out the whiskey."

"I really didn't know what to do about it," Cliff said. "It's strange how somebody so nice can do things that are wrong. I don't know what to say to him anymore. He lied to me. I hated that."

"I guess there's good and bad in all of us, Cliff. We have to take folks pretty much as they are. You don't have to like what Hoke did. That was wrong and his lying is wrong. But there's a lot of good in him, too. You can appreciate that and still feel that he's your friend."

Cliff thought about that. Hoke was so many things. He was wrong to make the whiskey but he had courage to confess it. He would tell a lie but he was man enough to walk straight into a trap when he knew that Ted was hurt. He was careless and carefree, sometimes irresponsible, but he wouldn't run away. It was true, when the chips were down he was a friend.

"He's been really good to me. I couldn't sleep after I found out about him. I worried and worried. I didn't want to tell on him."

"You handled it pretty well, Cliff. Better than I might have. You gave him a chance to make his own decision, but then you did what you had to do."

"I really didn't know what was right," said Cliff. "I was afraid he'd run away and I was so happy when I saw him fanning Ted."

Daddy crossed his arms on the table and looked across at Cliff. "Being a boy is often a hard and curious experience, Cliff," he said. "When you're growing up some days are bright and shiny as sunlight on Blue Hole Mill Pond, and some are darker than the inside of Jonah's whale." He sighed deeply. "Sometimes a thing that seems right to do turns out to be wrong, like when you didn't tell about Fast Buck. And sometimes a thing that seems wrong is really right—like telling about Hoke. When you're twelve it's hard to know which is which." Daddy looked out into the starlit night as if thinking beyond Cliff to his own boyhood.

In the silence that followed, Cliff's mind touched the painful quarrel he had had with Ted and, suddenly, in this moment of sharing with Daddy he wanted to talk about it.

"Ted wanted to tell about Hoke," he said. It was somehow difficult to tell Daddy about this and his words came with hesitation. "Ted said we had no right to protect Hoke and I got mad. We had a fuss."

"You had a fuss?"

Cliff nodded. "I told him he would not feel that way if Hoke was a white man. He said I told a black lie." The words were painful.

Daddy was silent for a long time. Cliff thought he might not have heard him. He wasn't sure he could say it over again. Then Daddy spoke.

"Being a boy is difficult, like I said, Cliff. And being a Negro boy is especially difficult. It takes a lot of patience and a lot of wisdom to handle all the problems that will come to you. The world you're growing up in will be different from the one that Mama and I have known and we want you to be able to live in that world without fear and with as few scars as possible."

He was quiet again for a moment and Cliff did not speak.

"You may run into a lot of fusses in your lifetime," Daddy continued finally. "Some of them will really hurt. We can't protect you from being hurt along the way, but we do want to help you face life with the kind of strength that will make you contribute something worthwhile to the society that you live in. We want you to fight for the things you think are right but we don't want you to go looking for a fight. We want you to be proud of what you are and not ashamed of who you are. We want you to face your world with courage and responsibility and to be able to work with all men—white men, black men—any kind of man—doing the very best job you know how to do, whatever it may be."

Cliff let Daddy's words sink into his mind, feeling the cool wind blow across his face.

"Ted said he didn't mean the words like they sounded," he said. "He didn't mean to call me black."

"Even if he had meant them, you have to face that fact, too, and we want you to be able to face it with pride. You are black and Ted is white. You start from that clean fact. You've got to live in a world like this, made up of white men and black men—some of them good, some of them bad and most of them a little bit of both. And men have to know how to give the best that's in them to make this world a good one."

Daddy sighed again. "It may mean that you have to try a little harder than some of the people you know— find extra courage. You'll have to be more honest, less sensitive to hurt, and more sensitive to what other people are thinking. In other words, you have to develop the good qualities within you so that they outweigh the bad."

Sitting there in the dim light Cliff thought about this a long time. "I guess, when you come right down to it, the good in Hoke outweighed the bad, didn't it, Daddy?"

"I guess you'd have to say that, Cliff. And that's why I was proud of you today. You were fair with Hoke, but you did what you had to do, and it seems to me that you straightened out your problem with Ted, too."

"I thought one time maybe Ted and I would never be friends again," said Cliff. "We never talked about me being a Negro before."

"It's probably better that you and Ted brought your differences out into the open," said Daddy. "But there's no point in fussing about it."

"I told him I was wearing a chip on my shoulder," said Cliff.

"Yes, I think you were and it's easy to do that when you feel that no one understands your problems. But if you can accept who you are and be proud of what you are, then you can hold up your head and meet Ted or any other boy on any level without apology."

Cliff looked at his daddy and felt a warm rush of pride. Daddy could really make you feel good and clean inside. He grinned a little.

"I feel like I just chewed off my paw," he said.

"You mean like the weasel?" Daddy said laughing.

"Sort of free," said Cliff.

He thought about all this later when Daddy had gone back into the living room and Mama had come out to help awhile. They sat on the floor for the four-o'clock feeding and watched the pony sink back down when he had finished the bottle. They were too tired to talk and the dim light shimmered before Cliff's eyes.

He looked at Mama who held the little pony's head in her lap. Her own head was tilted back against the screen wire that protected them from insects. Her eyes were closed.

"She looks so tired," Cliff thought, realizing this was the first time he had ever thought his mother looked tired. "She's pulling for the pony just like Daddy and I are. She really wants him to live. It really matters to her."

The thought pleased him and he smiled. The little foal had somehow made Mama seem a member of the farm family. He looked beyond her head at the streaks of dawn that were beginning to appear in the east and thought how long it had been since he had heard Cricket outside his window, with the same faint colors appearing in the sky—how many things had happened. He leaned his cheek against the screen and fastened his eyes on the pale eastern light. His stinging eyelids closed.

Moments later he woke up, frantic with fear that he had slept past the hour, but the hands of the clock had moved forward only fifteen minutes.

He thought about Ted in the hospital and wondered if he were asleep and comfortable. Ted would like hearing about the weasel's paw. He'd probably giggle in the funny way he had and he'd want to know all about the foal. Cliff put his hand on the pony feeling the heavy white mane and the sleek sides. The foal's breathing was light and shallow. He didn't stir.

It would be lonesome without Ted, but school would be starting soon. Cliff's thoughts lingered on that for a time. Maybe it would be easier in Jackson than it had been in some places. He would be meeting many new boys, but maybe the boys would be different. Maybe some of them would be like Ted. And then the thought occurred to Cliff. "Maybe I'm a little bit different, too. Maybe I know how to meet boys better. Maybe I can be a better friend because of knowing Ted. Maybe I can face facts with more courage."

And in that moment, staring out beyond the warm circle of light into the darkness, Cliff knew that he could. He knew the year ahead would be a better one. He knew he could face his teachers and his schoolmates with a new sense of pride in the kind of person he was. He could be honest without pretending. He could be fair. He could meet disappointment, accept hurts, and make mistakes without feeling that everybody in the world was against him. Daddy was right. He might have to try a little harder but he could do that, too. There must be lots of boys who would be friends. Of course, it would be hard to find anybody exactly like Ted—

He closed his eyes and thought of how it would be next summer when Ted came back—if only the little foal would live. The pony would be big enough to hitch to a cart— not old enough to ride, but then, he and Ted could still ride Cricket. His thoughts trailed off into nothingness—

He felt a gentle nudge at his arm and his eyes flew wide open. It was broad daylight and Mama was asleep, her head on one of the dining chairs. The colt was not stretched out on the floor beside her. Cliff felt the nudge again and turned to look. The little pony was standing up. Cliff stared in wonder.

"Mama," he cried out. "Look. Oh, look, Mama. He's up." Cliff stood up and the colt took a few steps, wobbling foolishly on his slender legs.

Mama's head came up with a jerk. She moved her stiff limbs slowly but she smiled, a smile still full of sleep but full of joyous triumph, too.

She got up quickly and stood looking down at the colt. "I'll go in and fill the bottle again," she said.

"Put in two ounces this time," Cliff said and then he ran to the back door leading into the house.

"Daddy," he called. "Come see. The pony's up. He can walk."

Daddy appeared at the dining-room door almost immediately and he watched while Cliff held the bottle toward the pony. The little colt grabbed it with his lips and sucked eagerly.

Paul and Wesley, still in pajamas, came stumbling out the back door to look. They laughed at the pony who stood on shaky legs with his little neck stretched out to reach the bottle that Cliff held.

"May I told the bottle now?" Paul asked.

Cliff laughed happily. "I guess you can," he said. He helped Paul hold it at the proper angle. Wesley walked over and put his hand on it, too.

"Now, the whole family has had a hand in helping to bring this pony around," said Cliff. His heart felt big and warm with the happiness that filled him. He looked at Mama and Daddy who stood together watching their three sons feed the pony. The eastern sky had softened to pure gold and the first rays of sunlight pierced the thin blue mist to touch the Morgan family.

They watched the little foal nurse until the milk was gone. He turned the nipple loose and lifted his head until his neck was arched as if stretching. His tiny ears pricked forward and his bright eyes regarded the three boys. As they watched, his little white tail twitched saucily.

"Hey, look at that," Daddy said. "I believe he's going to be a real crackajack pony."

Cliff looked at Daddy with sudden decision brightening his face.

"You've just named him, Daddy," he said.

"What's that?"

"I'm going to call him Crackajack."

"That's a perfect name," said Mama, coming out to set the table for breakfast. She paused with dishes in her hand and the five of them stood looking at Crackajack who took a few wobbly steps toward Cliff, then reconsidered. He dropped to his knees and stretched out to have another nap before his next feeding time.